CAMP SCARE

Also by Delilah S. Dawson

Mine

CAMP SCARE

DELILAH S. DAWSON

Delacorte Press

Text copyright © 2022 by D. S. Dawson
Jacket art copyright © 2022 by Matt Ryan Tobin

All rights reserved. Published in the United States
by Delacorte Press, an imprint of Random House Children's Books,
a division of Penguin Random House LLC, New York.

Delacorte Press is a registered trademark
and the colophon is a trademark
of Penguin Random House LLC.

Visit us on the Web! rhcbooks.com

Educators and librarians, for a variety of teaching tools,
visit us at RHTeachersLibrarians.com

Library of Congress Cataloging-in-Publication Data
Names: Dawson, Delilah S., author.
Title: Camp Scare / Delilah S. Dawson.
Description: First edition. | New York : Delacorte Press, [2022] |
Audience: Ages 8-12 years. | Summary: Bullied and lonely, Parker Nelson is
excited to make a new friend at camp, but then bad, unexplainable things
start happening to Parker's tormenters.
Identifiers: LCCN 2021036858 (print) | LCCN 2021036859 (ebook) |
ISBN 978-0-593-37326-2 (hardcover) | ISBN 978-0-593-37328-6 (ebook)
Subjects: CYAC: Bullying—Fiction. | Ghosts—Fiction. | Revenge—Fiction. |
Camps—Fiction. | LCGFT: Novels.
Classification: LCC PZ7.D323 Cam 2022 (print) | LCC PZ7.D323 (ebook) |
DDC [Fic]—dc23

The text of this book is set in 11.25 Apollo MT Pro.
Interior design by Jen Valero

Printed in the United States of America
10 9 8 7 6 5 4 3 2 1
First Edition

This book is dedicated to every kid who's ever been told:

- *you're a bit much*
- *maybe you could listen a little more and talk a little less*
- *you don't have to raise your hand to answer every question*
- *just be yourself and everybody will like you*
- *just ignore the bullies and they'll go away*

You are not alone.

1.

Finally—finally!—all of Parker Nelson's dreams were coming true.

The 102 on today's math test hadn't been a surprise, but getting paired up with *the* Cassandra DiVecchio for the big Language Arts project and then invited to her house to work on it? That was a huge score. Parker didn't need any help with the project—she was the biggest poetry nerd in her class and already had ideas—but she had been trying to break into the popular clique since kindergarten.

Okay, maybe that was an understatement.

Parker had been trying to break into *any* friend group ever since people started declaring their besties and inviting each other to slumber parties. She'd lived in the same house in the same town her entire life, gone to the same schools with the same kids, and yet it felt as if all of the friend groups had been established without her knowledge, as if there were no seats left in the musical chairs of friendship.

Sure, she could get a little braggy about her grades and had been told by several adults that she had a tendency to talk too much, too fast, mostly about herself, and not really give other kids a chance to say anything. And, yes, she was proud to be a teacher's pet and loved to spout weird facts whenever she could. But she thought she was, in general, a good person who would make a great friend, and she was trying harder to fit in. So far, she hadn't been able to crack the code, but she'd really been studying Cassandra and her crew and was starting to see where she'd been going wrong. After a trip to the outlet mall for new sneakers and her first attempt at eyeliner after multiple YouTube tutorials, Parker felt as ready as she'd ever be.

Her mom watched anxiously from the car as Parker hitched her backpack up on her shoulder—the cool kids never wore both straps—and walked up the curved stone sidewalk to Cassandra's house, or maybe *mansion* would be a better word. The house was so tall and white that it was almost blinding, and Parker wondered what it would be like to pack up everything she owned and pull up to a house like this, as Cassandra must have last year when she moved here from Tennessee and was immediately absorbed into KJ Worthington's highly selective lunch table, forming a trio along with KJ's second-in-command, Olivia Blanchard.

Giddy, her stomach full of butterflies, Parker rang the doorbell and glanced back at her mom, motioning for her to leave. Her mom gave her a thumbs-up, pointed at her cell phone, waved, and backed out of the driveway right as the big stained-glass door opened to reveal the third most popular girl in seventh grade.

Cassandra stood there looking a little uncertain, which was unusual for her. She had long, straight black hair and honey-gold eyes, and everything about her was pretty much perfect. Her style was careless—a big sweatshirt and ragged jean shorts, like everybody wore—but somehow, on her, it looked effortless and cool.

"Oh," Cassandra said, looking Parker up and down. "You look cute."

The hour Parker had spent with the straightening iron and her mom's makeup drawer must've worked, to get a compliment like that. She was smiling so hard that her face hurt. Her sweatshirt was almost exactly the same as the one Cassandra wore, which had to be a sign. "Thanks! I love your house."

"Come on in. You can leave your shoes here. My room's upstairs."

Cassandra's house was decorated like something from a magazine or a movie, like someone had professionally tossed blankets around and karate-chopped pillows right before Parker walked in. She left her shoes at the door and followed Cassandra's swinging ponytail, glad that she could ogle the house as much as she wanted behind Cassandra's back. On the way up the perfectly white stairs, she longed to pause and study all the framed black-and-white pics of Cassandra and her older sister, starting from when they were super tiny. It was a big surprise, learning that even Cassandra DiVecchio had had an awkward phase that involved chipmunk cheeks, braces, glasses, and horrible bangs.

When they reached Cassandra's room, Parker was again in awe. It was like the dressing room of a really fancy store, right down to the pink couch with furry white pillows. Parker tossed down her backpack and flopped onto the couch, grinning.

"So I was thinking we could do iambic pentameter," she started. "Like one of Shakespeare's poems, but—"

"Yeah, sure," Cassandra agreed, eyes glued to her phone. "But, hey. I forgot—my mom ordered this gourmet ice cream. Want to go downstairs and get some?"

Parker's jaw nearly dropped. Gourmet ice cream at Cassandra DiVecchio's house? She wanted to pinch herself but knew that sort of thing just made girls like Cassandra roll their eyes.

"Sure!" she said, hopping up off the couch. "Ice cream is always good. I had gelato once, and that was good, too, but it came with this really tiny spoon, which was weird. And there were no chunks. So I probably like ice cream better, because human beings are wired to enjoy digging up chunks. It's this anthropology thing—"

"Oh, totally. Come on." Cassandra smiled and nodded, but she seemed almost . . . nervous. Not like Parker's brand of loud, nervous energy—where she talked too much, too fast, and said weird things and made a fool of herself—but as if she was afraid of making someone mad. Maybe Cassandra's parents were really strict. Maybe her mom didn't want anyone to eat her gourmet ice cream. Parker hadn't heard a single sound in the huge house, but then again, the carpet was so thick it was like walking in snow.

Cassandra led her back downstairs and to the kitchen, where she pulled several pints of ice cream out of a huge freezer. Parker tried not to babble at her while they made sundaes in glass dishes, adding whipped cream and maraschino cherries.

"I didn't know you could just buy these at the store," Parker said, contemplating how many of the cherries she could reasonably dig out of the jar with her fork before it got weird.

"You can buy anything if you know where to get it." Cassandra hadn't taken as much ice cream, but then again, she could help herself any time she wanted while Parker might never have a chance like this again. "I have this weird uncle in Florida who once bought an eight-foot-long stuffed alligator."

"Like, a stuffed animal or an animal that's been stuffed? I mean, soft and fluffy or scaly and hard?"

"Big difference, right?" Cassandra laughed. "Scaly and hard. He still has his teeth. His name is Gerald." Before Parker could ask, she added, "The alligator is Gerald. My uncle is Robert."

"Also a big difference. Hopefully Robert also still has teeth, too."

When they laughed together, Parker had the realization that this might be the best moment of her life: laughing over weird facts with Cassandra DiVecchio while eating gourmet ice cream. Surely this project would make Cassandra see what a cool person Parker was, and maybe she'd get a coveted invite to the lunch table she shared with KJ and Olivia, and—

There was a thump from overhead, and Cassandra's eyes darted to the stairs before she turned back to Parker with a grin. "My dad was the chef of this really big hotel, and once a movie star ordered an ostrich egg, and they had to go find one at, like, midnight. And then he had to make the world's biggest omelet."

"Did he taste it? Because I read somewhere that ostrich eggs taste about the same as chicken eggs, although it depends on what they eat, because sometimes ostriches eat chicken feed and sometimes they eat bugs and lizards."

"Oh, he totally tasted it. Good chefs don't send out anything without tasting it. He said it tasted about the same, but they made him put salsa and all these veggies in it, so it kind of blurred the taste. What's the point, right? Just use twenty-four normal eggs if you're going to drench it in hot sauce."

"I always wondered what weird eggs tasted like."

Cassandra swirled her ice cream together. "I've had duck and quail. Duck eggs are very rich, and quail eggs are really teeny. We had them raw on sushi."

"You shouldn't eat raw eggs—" Parker started.

"Because salmonella, right? But most people who get sick from cookie dough actually get sick from the flour."

Parker was really getting excited, talking to Cassandra. They seemed to find the same sorts of things interesting. "I know! My dad and I play tons of trivia games, and that was one of the questions. Wait, how did you know that?"

"Like I said—my dad's a chef. And I watch *Jeopardy!* with my oma sometimes."

Parker took another bite of her sundae, wondering what made gourmet ice cream different from regular ice cream. Cassandra just nibbled at hers and definitely didn't eat with Parker's enthusiasm. She'd seemed really in tune with the conversation, but now she was acting distracted. When her phone buzzed in her back pocket, she startled and dropped her spoon, checking her text with a frown before cleaning up the mess.

"Everything okay?" Parker asked, because something was definitely wrong.

"Yeah, it's fine." Cassandra shook her head at the phone and put it in her pocket, where it continued to buzz. She poked at her ice cream, just moving it around listlessly until it was grayish soup.

"If, um, something's bothering you, uh, you can tell me if you want. I'm really good at keeping secrets," Parker said, well aware that this was only an assumption, as no one had ever told her a secret before.

Cassandra snorted and dumped her ice cream into the sink, running the faucet over it until it had disintegrated, which seemed like a waste of perfectly good ice cream. "No, it's fine. I mean, whatever."

Things became super awkward as Parker ate ice cream by herself in front of one of the most popular girls in school. It was as if a wall had come down and Cassandra was no longer paying any attention to her. She must've messed up somehow, as she always did. She ate faster, knowing full well she'd get an ice cream headache, and ended up dribbling a huge glop of chocolate sauce down the front of her new sweatshirt. Utterly dismayed, she scrounged up her cherries and put the empty dish in the sink, running water into it until it was mostly clean.

"Okay," she said, "so are you ready to get down to business? If you don't like Shakespeare, we could do Emily Dickinson. She's one of my favorites." When Cassandra grimaced, Parker added, "I mean, it's okay. Like, for poetry."

Parker was actually really, really into poetry, but she was pretty certain that Cassandra was not. Parker usually ended up pulling the full weight in group projects, but this time she didn't mind. Maybe if Cassandra got to know her, she'd see that Parker was cool in her own way.

"I kind of like Poe," Cassandra said, soft and a little hopeful. "Like, 'The Raven'?"

"Yeah, that could work!" Ideas swirled through Parker's mind like a cloud of black birds around a tower as she imagined the ways they could combine poetry, art, and maybe a skit? The poetry project was for a big grade, and while she knew she'd have an A in the class, she loved any excuse to show off.

Parker bolted for the stairs, fingers twitching for her journal and pen.

"Where are you going?" Cassandra asked, hurrying behind her.

"To get my stuff." Parker pounded up the stairs, excited

about the directions this project could go. "We could make a papier-mâché raven, maybe a bust of Athena. I've got a big piece of cardboard that could be a door—"

"Parker, wait—"

"We could wear togas!" Parker called back to her, humming with possibilities. "Like, we could be statues. We could be statues of Athena! Pallid busts of Pallas!"

The door to Cassandra's room was closed, which was weird, as it had been open when they left, but Parker assumed other people lived in the house, or maybe they had one of those cats that could open and close doors.

"Parker, stop!"

Parker did not stop. She couldn't. She threw open the door and—

The whole world froze, one gigantic pause button.

KJ and Olivia were there, using their phones to take pictures of—

Oh, please no.

No.

Parker's journal.

It was on the floor, open to a poem she'd written, one she never wanted anyone to see.

The contents of her backpack were strewn around, but of course they'd gone for the most personal thing, the thing Parker had never actually shown to another living person. She wanted to throw up, ice cream creeping up her throat. She wanted to punch the wall. She wanted to sink into the soft white carpet.

KJ Worthington looked up at her, blue eyes sparkling, perfect red hair dangling over Parker's most private and personal thoughts. "Oh, Parker, hi," she cooed, like they were just passing in a hallway. "Your poetry is soooooo good."

Olivia flicked through her phone and stood, mockingly reciting words that made Parker see red: "I'm Nobody! Not like you. / You're so cool you forget other people exist, too. / There's more of us than there are of you. / I'm telling you this because it's true."

KJ and Olivia howled with laughter, and KJ waved her phone where Parker could see it open to a social media site that her mother wouldn't let her use. "It's already got five hundred likes, and it's only been up for two minutes!" KJ screeched.

Parker turned to glare at Cassandra, who stood behind her on the stairs, her arms crossed as if she was trying to disappear.

"You did this on purpose," Parker said, the words rushing out. She felt sick.

Cassandra angrily waved at her room. "C'mon, Parker. Why would you just carry something like that with you where anyone could find it?"

"That's like asking someone who just got burglarized why they just have a house out in the open," Parker shot back.

KJ was taking more pics of the journal—of some original characters Parker had designed—so Parker lunged into the room and snatched the book from her hand. KJ and Olivia laughed as Parker stuffed it into her backpack, then awkwardly rammed all her other books and binders on top, wrinkling up everything and probably ruining all sorts of important work.

"Give me the phone," she said, shoving her open hand in KJ's face.

"Uh, no thanks." Instead, KJ used her phone to take a pic of Parker that had to be unflattering.

"Then delete the pictures."

Olivia crossed her arms. "Or what?"

There was no "or what." Short of attacking them, there wasn't anything Parker could do, and they all knew it.

"Did you guys plan this?" Parker asked, looking from KJ to Olivia to Cassandra. "Did you just . . . wake up today and decide to ruin my life?"

"Oh, you do that perfectly well on your own," KJ said with an eye roll.

"Cassandra said you were coming over, and we wanted to have some fun," Olivia added with an annoying little shrug, as if that made it okay.

Cassandra said nothing, just stared straight ahead, face red and arms crossed.

"Thanks for the ice cream," Parker snapped, pushing past Cassandra and running down the stairs.

"But what about your group project?" KJ called with the faux sweetness for which she was known. "Aren't you going to overdo it as usual and have, like, dancing poodles and fireworks?"

"Just because you do the bare minimum and get Cs doesn't

mean there's something wrong with caring, you ignoramus!"
Parker shouted back. "Not that you even know what that word
means!"

The only response was laughter.

Parker had trouble getting the front door unlocked but
no trouble slamming it. Outside, she marched to a bench by
the driveway and slumped beside her lumpy backpack as she
texted her mom, asking for an immediate pickup.

Parker had thought all her dreams were coming true, but
really, it was just the beginning of a nightmare.

2.

Two months later...

It was June, and with school out, Parker was no longer forced on a daily basis to suffer the ramifications of what she called the Ice Cream Incident. KJ and Olivia certainly hadn't let her forget, and there wasn't much the school could do about anonymously posted screenshots of Parker's poetry and art, much less the terrible photo of her, red-faced and crying with chocolate sauce on her shirt. It was like playing whack-a-mole: as soon as the powers that be forced one kid to delete it, it popped up somewhere else. Parker still wasn't allowed to have social media on her phone, but kids constantly shoved their screens in her face, and her dad spent an hour on his laptop every night trying to shut down the new additions.

"Trust me, they're just jealous," her school counselor had said. "Uncreative people always wish they could be like you."

But Parker knew the truth. They were mean girls, and

they'd done a mean thing, and for all the school's antibullying posters, there really wasn't anything anyone could do. She'd kept her head down and basically tried to disappear, eating her lunch in the bathroom and hurrying through the halls and sitting as close to the teacher as possible in every class and right behind the bus driver. Now that seventh grade was officially over, she had one goal: to reinvent herself over the summer and start eighth grade as a new, improved, unbullyable version of Parker Nelson.

That's why she was currently in the middle of nowhere.

Her mom's SUV bumped down the long dirt road, tree branches occasionally scratching along the roof. The directions said that once they'd turned off the highway at the big wooden sign, they were just two miles away from Camp Care.

"Are you sure you'll be okay?" her mom asked again, leaning nervously over the steering wheel. "It's so far away, and you've never been away overnight before, and—"

"It's going to be great," Parker said firmly, arms wrapped around her duffel bag.

In what felt like a consolation prize for being bullied, the school district had awarded her a scholarship to one of the best overnight camps in the state, a bucolic place known for its commitment to emotional health and its zero-tolerance stance toward bullying. According to the brochure and the bare-bones website, Camp Care had been open for over sixty years and offered dozens of opportunities to learn new skills and make forever friends in a beautiful outdoor setting. Best of all, it was far enough away that no one from her old school would be there, which meant Parker could test-drive what it would be like to be completely unknown.

No one at Camp Care had memorized her poems. No one would call her Nobody and laugh. No one would sarcastically tell her she was a great artist and ask her to sign doctored copies of her drawings. And because no phones were allowed at camp, no one could take yet more embarrassing pictures of her and share them on social media as memes.

Here, she really was nobody. But maybe she could become somebody better.

She would make friends with other girls, have inside jokes and trade friendship bracelets. They'd pose for pictures with their arms around each other's necks or maybe grinning in a pyramid. She'd flirt with the boys at the campfire, maybe even have her first kiss at the dock by the lake. With a new wardrobe and no past, it was going to be incredible. And instead of talking over everyone and blabbing her weird facts and sucking up to the counselors, she was going to do what people like Cassandra DiVecchio did: be quiet and stylish and cool, agree with the other girls, and generally try to be involved without standing out in any way. If it would help her make friends, she was willing to go completely against her personality. After all, what did she have to lose? Her old method of trying to make friends had been a lifelong failure.

Up ahead, the forest opened to a wide green clearing. A big wooden building with huge gleaming windows sat prominently,

winged by staggered rows of nearly identical brown cabins.
Trails led off into the woods like something out of a fairy tale.
The sun filtered down through the leaves, its golden beams
picking out the words carved on a wooden arch:

CAMP CARE, Est. 1956

Parker's mom pulled into an open space in the field, and
Parker looked around at all the other kids unloading bags
and trunks from their cars. Everyone looked happy, and most
of the kids were wearing the same outfit, navy blue gym shorts
and soft gray T-shirts emblazoned with the words CAMP CARE.
Her own duffel was full of new clothes modeled on what the
popular girls wore. Her jean shorts were perfectly ragged; her
tees were oversized and either tie-dyed or delicate pastels;
her sneakers were the same black Nikes everyone back home
wore. Sure, she missed her old wardrobe of unicorn shirts and
patterned leggings, but she was willing to do pretty much anything to avoid getting bullied again.

Mom grabbed her suitcase, and Parker picked up her backpack and duffel. They took their places in the line that led to
three cheerful older teens at a table labeled CHECK IN. As they
waited their turn, Parker watched kids spot one another and
scream and dash up for hugs and excited conversation. Lots
of these kids seemed to know each other and have that kind of
easy confidence that she had never quite been able to manage.
She had hoped that everyone here would be on the same foot-
ing with her, but the more she looked around, the more she

began to suspect that the other campers had played their own game of musical friend chairs long before she'd even heard of Camp Care. She was starting to get nervous.

Finally, it was their turn at the table.

"Hi! You must be one of our new campers!" The girl's name tag read COUNSELOR MAEVE, and she seemed to Parker like the kind of person who could talk only in exclamation points. "What's your name!"

Parker's mom nodded at her encouragingly. "I'm Parker Nelson."

Maeve flipped through her clipboard and smiled. "Here you are! You're going to be in Possum cabin with me!" Maeve held out a name tag, and Parker stuck it to her shirt.

She sensed that an energetic response was expected, so she said, "Cool! I actually really like possums. Did you know they're the only marsupial in North America and that their body temperature is too low for them to carry rabies?"

As soon as it was out of her mouth, Parker regretted it. She had to be more chill.

But Maeve's enthusiasm was unabated. "Sure did! I was in Possum cabin myself when I was your age, so I know all my possum facts! Now let's make sure you have everything you need! One set of sheets and a pillow?"

"Check."

"Toiletries, undergarments, sunblock, bug spray, bathing suit?"

"Check."

Maeve kept going down the list, and Parker was proud to note that she had everything necessary.

"Seven Camp Care uniform sets?"

"Wait. What?"

Maeve pointed at her worn gray T-shirt. "We all wear the uniform, because we're all equal and on the same team! It's part of what makes Camp Care so special!"

Parker looked at her mom, who was equally confused. Neither of them had gotten that message from the brochure. "I just brought regular shirts and jean shorts."

That finally made Maeve's smile waver. "Well, you can buy what you need at the camp commissary in Friendship Hall. All your other outfits can go home with Mom. No big deal!"

Parker grimaced. It *felt* like a big deal. She'd convinced her mom that new clothes were absolutely necessary, and now her mom had to buy a whole bunch of newer new stuff. Her dad was going to be annoyed; he didn't like surprises and wasn't totally on board with the camp anyway. He always said that if Parker just kept on being her best self, people would eventually take notice. He had not, Parker reminded him constantly, ever been a teen girl.

"Aside from the uniforms, it sounds like you're all ready. Stop by the commissary, and then take everything to Possum cabin, which is to the right of Friendship Hall. My cocounselor, Jasmine, is there to help you get settled. We're going to have a great summer!"

Parker's excitement had dimmed a bit. She hated starting out with a faux pas, even if her counselor was the only one who knew. She hurried back to the car and threw her suitcase into the back seat.

"Are you sure there's nothing in there you need?" her mom asked.

"No, all the boring stuff is in my backpack and duffel."

Her mom remained quiet, as she often did when Parker got upset, and Parker marched toward the big building behind the registration tables, which had to be Friendship Hall. For an old camp, this structure looked unexpectedly new, with shiny wood and big windows and bright lights. Long tables with benches and the baked-in scent of pizza removed any doubt that this was the cafeteria, and Parker was pleased to see a stage at one end with red velvet curtains. There weren't any other parents or kids inside—they must've all received the memo about uniforms. She led her mom toward the open double doors under a sign reading COMMISSARY. The overly tan old guy sitting behind the cash register had long white hair in a ponytail but looked like he ran twice a day for fun.

When he looked up from the paperback he was reading, Parker's mom told him they needed to purchase uniforms. He smiled and started pulling shirts down from the cubbies on the wall, measuring them against Parker until they'd found the right size.

"Uniforms are part of the Camp Care way," he said with

pride as he folded seven shirts and seven pairs of shorts into neat stacks. "Same shirt since 1956, when my grandparents founded the camp—we even use the same font."

Parker looked around the building doubtfully. "This place doesn't look like it was built in 1956."

A dark look passed over the man's face. "No, this particular building is from the eighties. Some parts of the camp are older than others." His grin returned, mostly. "We have to keep things up to code of course. And the beds are much more comfortable than they were when I was a kid. I'm Barry Fogarty, by the way. Executive director of the camp and wilderness skills teacher extraordinaire." He held out his hand, and Parker and her mom each shook it. "The kids call me Foggy."

When Parker saw the total for her uniforms, she flinched. Mom silently paid it, and Parker promised herself she'd do extra chores when she got back home next week. Foggy put all the uniforms into an old paper bag.

"See you at the campfire, Parker!" he called as they left.

"Thanks!" she called back. Back home, she might've told him how pretty the camp was and how happy she was to be here, but the new version of Parker was determined not to be a suck-up.

She was silent as they carried her new uniforms across Friendship Hall and back outside, where she missed the kiss of air-conditioning. She walked quickly toward the cabins on the hall's right, her anxiety growing. Camp, so far, was not matching her daydreams, and there weren't many parents out here, beyond the check-in table. The cabins spread out among the trees were all identically built and painted, but their decorations were slightly different. Each one was named after an animal— all harmless ones, Parker noted, no wolves or eagles here—with birdhouses, dream catchers, mobiles, and artwork all over. Possum cabin was a little far off, partially hidden by the shadows of the thick trees, in the back row of the staggered line.

"Are you going to be okay?" her mom asked for possibly the hundredth time.

"I'll be fine," Parker replied, because she had to be. Maybe things weren't going to plan, but she was here, and she was going to see it through. Even if KJ, Olivia, and Cassandra never knew, she felt like wimping out of camp would somehow just confirm that she was the babyish dork they assumed her to be.

She could hear laughter and shrieks coming from Possum cabin's open door, so she dropped her bags and stopped. "Bye, Mom. I love you," she said quietly.

"I'm just not sure—this seems . . ." Her mom trailed off. "Are you sure? I'm just so worried about you." When her mom reached for her face, Parker stepped around to give her a side hug.

"It's going to be great. I'll see you next Sunday."

Her mom's eyes were full of tears—of course, because Parker had never been to a slumber party or been away from her parents for longer than it took to go to school. The camp was really strict about phones and screens, so she hadn't brought any tech at all. Unless there was an emergency, she wouldn't talk to her mom for a full week. Tears sprang to her eyes, and she dashed them away.

She could do this. *She could.*

She picked up all her stuff, including the bag of uniforms her mom had been carrying, and marched toward her cabin.

"Love you, honey," her mom called.

"Love you, too," she called back, softly, but she didn't turn around, because if she did, she might chicken out.

It was cooler under the trees, despite the summer heat. The ground had been cleared and beaten down by years of feet, but weeds and vines snaked here and there as if they wanted her to trip in front of her new bunkmates. Right before she got to the door, she put her shoulders back and pasted on a confident smile. These kids didn't know Parker Nelson, and she was determined that her first impression would be a good one.

She stepped through the open door and looked around for the other counselor, Jasmine. All the shrieking stopped, and nine girls stopped smacking each other with pillows to stare at her instead.

"Ooh, a new girl!" one called.

"Fresh meat!" squealed another.

"I thought it was just us again," complained a third.

"Parker Nelson?" said a fourth voice, a voice Parker knew.

There, holding a pillow, frozen in the middle of what looked to be a movie-ready pillow fight, was Cassandra DiVecchio.

3.

Parker was pretty sure all the air had been sucked out of the cabin.

How could Cassandra possibly be here?

Camp Care was four hours from their town. It wasn't the sort of posh place rich girls like Cassandra flocked to. No makeup, no fancy clothes, no technology. Parker had never even heard of it until they received a letter from the school board. This place should've been entirely off the grid, like it existed in its own little world, cut off from embarrassing moments in the past.

And yet the main witness to Parker's embarrassing past was standing right there.

For a long moment, they just stared at each other, and Parker was surprised by what she saw. Cassandra's hair wasn't smooth and straight as glass—it was wavy, pushed back behind her ears, messy but not in the stylish way. She wasn't wearing any makeup or jewelry, but she was wearing glasses. And she looked just as horrified as Parker did.

"You must be Parker," said a lanky older teen with cute Afro puffs as she got up from a bottom bunk. She walked over, smiling warmly. "I'm Jasmine, one of the counselors. You got the last bunk, I'm afraid." She pointed to the top bunk, just above where she'd been curled up with a book. "Hope you're not afraid of heights."

"It'll be fine. Hi." Parker wasn't sure what to do, so she just stood there, arms trembling under the weight of all her stuff. For once, she was speechless.

"So these are your bunkmates. They're regulars—and a Girl Scout troop, back home. Addison, Sydney, Cassie, Charlotte, Kaylee, Zoe, Hanna, Emma, Rosemary." She pointed at each girl in turn. "Say hi, Possums!"

"Hi!" the girls sang back. Everyone looked excited to meet her . . . except Cassandra.

"Before you make your bed, you need to get into uniform. You can drop your bags in here and go change in the bathroom if you want privacy," Jasmine said. "But they want everyone in uniform as soon as possible. You brought uniforms, right?"

Parker nodded, put down her bags, and pulled out a tee and shorts. She definitely wanted privacy, with Cassandra around. They'd passed the communal bathrooms on their way to the cabin, and she wasn't sure how she felt about having to cross the darker parts of the forest at night if she had to pee. But she wasn't going to show any fear—not in front of new people, and especially not in front of Cassandra. All nine girls watched her silently as she hurried outside and jogged toward the bathroom. Maybe they'd be friendlier when she was in her matching uniform.

The girls' bathroom was in the center of the staggered line of cabins, nestled among the trees. Toilet stalls were to the left, sinks in the middle, and shower stalls to the right. For all that it looked new(er) and clean(ish), it had a definite smell, and the floor seemed as if it would be perpetually wet. Parker was the only one in there, so she quickly stepped into a toilet stall and struggled out of her tee and cutoffs and into the uniform, which felt scratchy and stiff. Everyone else's uniform looked soft and comfy, but apparently that took time. Even though she'd done everything in her power to fit in here, she was already way off the mark. Again, other kids just seemed to possess information she hadn't received.

The other girls, she'd noticed, didn't tuck in their shirts, so she didn't tuck in hers. She swatted at her hair in the mirror, but it just wouldn't lie right.

"So stupid," she muttered.

The fluorescent lights overhead flickered, something somewhere dripped, and the door to the last stall creaked open. Parker bent over, looking for feet, but no one was there. The building had open windows just over head height, so there was a nice breeze that probably made the door move. Still, she made a mental note not to drink too much water before bed, because if a bathroom was creepy at noon, it was going to be seriously terrifying at midnight.

As she walked back to Possum cabin, she saw kids sitting here and there, chatting or calling each other's names and running up for hugs. Everyone seemed so comfortable and happy to be there—except Parker. Between the uniforms and finding out she was in Cassandra's cabin, she felt just as awkward as she did back home.

But wait. Cassandra had been kind of nice when they were eating ice cream. Maybe she was just mean when she was around KJ and Olivia. Maybe here they could be friends. Parker pasted on a smile as she stepped back into her cabin, ready to win the other girls over.

Except—the moment she walked in the door, they all glared at her. They'd been curious and surprised when she first arrived, but now they looked angry and suspicious. Parker focused on Cassandra, but she quickly turned away and bent to paw through her bag.

"So what are we doing today?" Parker asked.

No one answered at first. Parker looked to Jasmine, but she had on headphones and was bopping her head to an old-fashioned portable CD player as she read her book.

"Free time until camp meeting and dinner at seven," one girl finally said—Addison, according to her name tag. She was tall and athletic with tan skin and blond hair and seemed like the kind of person other kids looked to for leadership.

"It's my first time here," Parker confessed. "So, I mean . . . do we just hang out here until then, or are there other choices?"

A pale girl with a tight white-blond French braid hugged her backpack to her chest and shook her head. Her name tag read SYDNEY. "Do you mean, when are we going to leave all our stuff here and unprotected so you can take it? Because that's not how things work at Camp Care. Stay away from my bunk."

Parker looked from girl to girl, mystified. There had to be some kind of misunderstanding. "What do you mean? I don't want your stuff. I just want to hang out or whatever."

"Yeah, right," said a third girl. "Let's go to the lake. Jasmine will stay here and watch everything, right?"

"Good call," Addison agreed. "The lake it is."

All the other girls stood up and cast suspicious glances at Parker as they stowed their bags and packs under their beds or in the dressers between the bunks. Cassandra was the only one who wouldn't look Parker's way.

As they filed out the door, Parker asked, "Can I come, too?"

"You can go wherever you want as long as you stay on camp property," Addison said. "Just don't go beyond the big fence. Until you know your way around, you don't want to get too far. The woods can be pretty freaky, and you'll definitely get lost." She shook her head sadly, as if she was somehow already disappointed with Parker, and left.

Soon it was just Parker and Jasmine, who wasn't paying any attention to her at all. The other girls had gone out of their way to not invite Parker along, but as Addison said, she could go wherever she pleased. Maybe there were nicer people in other cabins. She made her bed up neatly and put the rest of her things in the last dresser, wondering what had made the other girls so hostile. Sure, they all seemed to know each other, but their mood had changed so quickly.

There was only one answer: Cassandra.

She must've told her friends about how unpopular Parker was, maybe recited Parker's stupid poem for them and explained that she was the school pariah. And it sounded as if she'd also told them Parker was a thief. That had to be why they were being so terrible—because Cassandra couldn't stop being a bully for one single week.

After a few moments of silence in the cabin with nothing to do but listen to Jasmine hum, Parker couldn't stand it anymore. She went outside and watched to see what everyone else was doing. There were several dirt paths into the woods and connecting to other buildings, but there were no signs, and she hadn't seen a map. Literally everyone else seemed to know what they were doing and where they were going, and yet again, she felt like a little baby who hadn't received the rule book. The kids running around on their own seemed to be maybe eight and older, although there were some younger kids sitting in circles with their counselors playing games. There weren't any clocks she could see, and she began to wonder how anyone knew what time it was and when they were supposed to be anywhere. The whole place felt aggressively mysterious, as if it had been specifically designed to confuse and embarrass her.

Finally, sick of standing there and very well aware that people were staring, Parker decided to follow the sound of voices and laughter toward the biggest, most obvious trail. The path was hard-packed dirt, and her brand-new Nikes were already taking on its dusty red hue. It was kind of pretty, how the path forged through the forest under dappled sunlight, the trees meeting overhead. She saw birdhouses and bat houses and fairy houses hanging everywhere among the branches and on the trunks, all handmade with various degrees of success. Clay stepping-stones and sculptures lined the path. After a few minutes of walking, the trail opened up to reveal an enormous lake shining in the sun. There were multiple docks, rows of canoes and kayaks and paddleboards, little cabins along the shore, and a floating platform in the middle of the lake that kids in bathing suits were lounging on. Several counselors in red swimsuits kept watch from tall chairs, the sun glinting off their sunglasses. A woman in her thirties with a perky ponytail and tennis visor stood by one of the cabins, arms crossed as she surveyed her domain with satisfaction.

The lake was so big that its edges disappeared into the trees. Parker gave a little shiver. She'd Googled this lake and learned that it wasn't natural but had once been a valley, and that a few small towns and farms had been abandoned before the area was purposefully flooded. Somewhere under all that water were homes, barns, cars, and cemeteries, just sitting there, rotting in the impenetrable darkness. And even if they weren't anywhere near this happy beach, there were logs and rocks and turtles and crayfish, all sorts of slimy things and creatures just living their lives underwater. She'd never really liked the ocean, and the lake was something she wanted to like but . . . well, it was going to take some time. At least she was an adept swimmer, even if all her time in the water had been spent in pools.

She spotted her cabinmates lounging on one of the docks, their shoes lined up on the gray boards and their legs dangling into the water. They had already spotted her and were whispering among themselves. She had to win them over, or at least make things less awkward—they were going to be together for the next seven days, after all. Pulling back her shoulders and putting on what she hoped was an easy smile, she strode across the sand and onto the dock. Addison stood and hurried to meet her, leaving wet footprints on the boards.

"So you're not allowed on the dock until you've taken a swim test," she said firmly but not unkindly. "We all passed ours years ago. If you want to come on the dock today, you have to put on one of the life jackets, but they're pretty gross."

Parker peered around her at the group. A few of them were smirking. Cassandra's face was as blank as glass.

"How do I take the swim test?" she asked.

"They'll do it sometime tomorrow, whenever we're scheduled for lake time."

Parker had only ever swum in the neighborhood pool and

at the water park, but she would swim in the lake if it meant she wasn't an outcast. "Okay, so where are the life jackets?"

The tall girl pointed at a rack of faded orange jackets near the canoe racks. "Like I said, they're gross."

Parker could practically smell the mildew from here. "I'm Parker, by the way—"

"I know. I'm Addison."

"Look, I don't know what Cassandra told you, but—"

Addison shook her head. "I've known Cassie since I was six. I met you ten minutes ago. Sorry, but I'm going to listen to Cassie until you prove her wrong." Addison raised her eyebrows before turning back to the now forbidden dock and her friends.

Parker tucked that away for later—whether it was through camp or somewhere else, Cassandra had known Addison and maybe the whole group longer than she'd even been at Parker's school. No wonder they just believed whatever lies she was spreading. Parker wanted to stomp down the dock and confront Cassandra, but she could now see what she was up against. These girls weren't going to believe her just because she called Cassandra a liar. All she could do was stick around, be friendly and helpful, and, like Addison said, prove their assumptions wrong. For now, she couldn't get close to them— literally.

She checked out the life vests, but Addison was right—she didn't want to put one on until she had to. They smelled like old, dusty mushrooms coated in tuna juice and left in the sun for ten years. No one else around the lake was wearing one, which meant she'd stick out like a sore thumb. The dock—and the girls she wanted to impress, who were sitting on it—were utterly out of reach.

Hands on her hips, she looked around the idyllic lakeside beach. She was the only camper who was alone. Everyone else was with a pal or a group, splayed out in the sun with arms around necks and feet kicked up over legs like puppies in a pile. Parker's heart ached to be part of that kind of comfortable camaraderie. It hurt to always be on the outside of it. So she turned away and followed the path back into the woods. It was darker under the trees, with forest noises she wasn't used to, rustles and snaps and sighs. She was almost certain someone was following her, but when she stopped, the other footsteps stopped, too.

"Hello?" she called.

When no one answered, she felt ridiculous, so she put on a burst of speed and hurried back toward the main campus.

She passed cabins with open doors filled with the burble of voices. There was an arts and crafts cabin, a STEM cabin, a music cabin emitting the trills of recorders as if it was full of baby birds. Parker glanced in each door but saw the same thing again and again: groups of happy kids who looked like photos out of a brochure. In her secret heart, she longed to find a cabin with just one companionless kid or even a sympathetic-looking adult, but she continued to be the only person experiencing even the tiniest drop of obvious loneliness.

When she reached Friendship Hall, she finally found a building full of silence—or, at least, a place that wasn't filled with happy kids whose very existence made her burn with jealousy. Cafeteria workers were busy preparing food, but the tables were empty, and that lack of extroversion felt welcoming. She pushed the glass door open, appreciating the purr of air-conditioning and determined to find something to do inside.

The commissary where she'd bought her uniforms was open, the same old guy perched on a stool with his glasses low on his nose as he flipped through paperwork. Maybe she would've liked to talk to a weird art teacher or friendly librarian, but she didn't have much to say to the camp director, so she headed for a matching set of French doors on the opposite side of the hall under a sign reading MUSEUM.

The lights were off, but big glass windows allowed sunlight to filter in, giving the room a feeling of permanent twilight, for all that it was only five o'clock or so. The walls were covered in photographs, artwork, and plaques, and display tables held dioramas, sculptures, and a few grubby taxidermy animals that had to be older than the guy in the commissary. The stuffed bear posed in front of the window had faded to the color of wet straw, and the snapping turtle looked like kids had been rubbing his shell since the age of the dinosaurs. Their glass eyes—and the eyes of the stuffed squirrel, skunk, fox, and otter—gleamed in the low light as if they might blink if she looked away.

Parker started on the left-hand wall and swiftly realized that she had started in the right place, as the artifacts had been hung in chronological order, according to the dates on their title cards. The very first frame held a printed brochure for the opening of Camp Care in 1956, back when it was all boys. The black-and-white photo beside it was so culturally inappropriate that it made Parker grimace: dozens of boys, all of them white, wearing face paint and feather headdresses beside a totem pole. There were newspaper clippings, a photo of a boy proudly holding a huge catfish, a decent sketch of the original director clearly done by a talented child.

As Parker moved along the wall, Camp Care evolved. Girls were allowed in, and more kids of color began to appear. A fresh-faced married couple in their twenties were announced as codirectors. The camp won awards and grants. Kids who'd gone here went on to do great things. A counselor rescued a kid from drowning; the camp director performed the Heimlich maneuver on a kid who'd choked on a piece of hot dog. Everything was positive and sunny, just like all those happy kids at the lake right now.

But Parker began to notice something odd. None of the buildings in the photos looked anything like Friendship Hall or the cabins she'd seen. The entrance sign was completely different. Even the images of the lake seemed off. She stood in front of a photo from the early eighties that showed the main hall and lines of cabins but all shaped and placed just a little differently.

"Reading up on our history, huh?"

Parker whirled around to find Director Fogarty standing there. He was smiling and friendly, and Parker knew that even if she wasn't generally liked or accepted by other kids, she was excellent with authority figures. Maybe the camp director—Foggy, he'd said the kids called him—would have some insight on the best way to make new friends here, especially considering there appeared to be a set of rules she'd never received.

"It's really interesting," she said. "It looked so different back then."

"That's because it *was* different." Foggy walked to the opposite wall, took down a photo, and brought it over to compare to the one Parker had been studying. "We rebuilt everything in 1989."

Parker compared the two photos, pleased that she'd been correct. "Why?"

Foggy didn't answer immediately. When Parker looked at him, his eyes seemed far away, his head hanging. He looked much older in that moment. "Nothing lasts forever," he finally said, turning away to replace the newer photo across the room. "It just wasn't safe anymore." He returned to her side and took a deep breath, putting on what seemed to Parker like a forced smile. "Besides, now we have air-conditioning. Believe me, Camp Care is better than ever."

It seemed like he wanted her to say something, so she said, "It's really beautiful here."

He put a hand on her shoulder. "Say, why aren't you out with your cabin? We don't see many loners around here. Camp Care is all about making friends for life."

Maybe it was because they were the only people around, or maybe it was because he was the only person so far who'd shown any kindness to her at all, but Parker couldn't stop herself from blurting out the truth.

"The other girls in my cabin are already friends, and they don't want to let me into their clique."

Foggy squeezed her shoulder, making her wince. "Are they bullying you? We have a zero-tolerance policy here, and I need to know if there's a problem."

Tears sprung into Parker's eyes. Her school had a zero-tolerance policy against bullies, too, but it couldn't protect anyone against outright shunning, and neither could Foggy. "It's not bullying. They just don't like me. I think someone spread a rumor about me."

The old man's fingers loosened, and he smiled. "Not my Camp Care kids! I know it's easy to feel like an outsider since most kids have been coming here since they were tiny. We let in the children of alumni first and have a waiting list as long as my leg, so we just don't get a lot of new campers. I'm sure they're a little leery, but you'll win 'em over. And if you don't, come talk to me, and I'll sort it out. I bet by tomorrow night, you'll all be best friends!"

He almost sounded like a car commercial, and Parker's gut felt as if it'd been scooped out with a melon baller. Of course he couldn't—or wouldn't—help. It was his camp, and he wanted everyone to be friends, and so they must be fine. Maybe he thought that if he kept talking about it in an overly cheerful, rehearsed way, he could make everyone else believe it, too. But not her.

"Thanks," she said, focusing on the next news clipping on the wall.

"Atta girl." Foggy gently punched her in the arm and left.

Unbelievably, his attempt at kindness had only made her feel worse.

At least the written word had never let Parker down. She had a couple of hours to kill before the camp meeting, whatever that was, and she was already here, so she decided to read everything she could about Camp Care. Maybe she'd find some insider knowledge that would help her discover her path.

She never found a list of rules, although she did find the lyrics to several campfire singalong songs that might help her later, which she attempted to commit to memory. She also found a complicated hand-drawn map full of pushpins, showing where all the cabins were, plus the chain-link fence Addison had mentioned—not that she could possibly remember it just by staring at it.

There was one odd thing she noticed, though, one thing she wished she'd known to ask Foggy about.

There wasn't a single thing from 1988. No group photographs, no newspaper clippings, no artwork. It just went from 1987 to 1989.

As if, for Camp Care, the entire year had never existed.

4.

At seven o'clock, someone played a trumpet, badly, over a speaker system to signal the camp meeting. Parker tried to muster her pluck. Maybe she just needed to look outside her cabin for friends. Surely there was someone else who didn't quite fit in, or who was new and hadn't yet found their place. With over a hundred kids here, she couldn't be the only square peg trying to fit into a round hole.

She watched from the door of the museum, waiting to see who would filter into the main hall. Unfortunately, the counselors were already waiting at their tables, gesturing to the kids in their cabins as they crowded through the open doors. When Jasmine waved to her, she reluctantly joined the rest of Possum cabin at their table. The girls all spread out, taking up as much room as possible and eyeing her with suspicion, but Jasmine scooched over and patted the bench beside her. Parker sat, feeling as if everyone else was moving as fast as a hummingbird's wings while she was stuck in slow motion.

"Did you hit the lake?" Jasmine asked.

"Yeah, it was pretty," Parker said, because she knew that telling Jasmine she was being shunned would only result in more punishment from the other girls.

Foggy stood on the stage at the far end of the cafeteria, beaming, as he waited for everyone to settle down.

"Welcome, everyone, to Camp Care!" he boomed.

"Thanks, Foggy!" the campers boomed back.

"We're gonna have a great summer!"

"Yes we are!"

"I'm glad to be your friend!"

"And I'm glad to be yours!"

Parker seemed to be the only one who didn't know the right words, and so far, no one seemed glad to be her friend. Foggy went into a welcome speech full of inside jokes, and Parker mostly tuned out. She scanned the room for interesting people, looking for kids who seemed different or lonely, but it was overwhelming. When everyone wore exactly the same clothes, it was hard to see what kind of people they were. There were no preppy pastels or morbid goths, no expensive purses or cheap backpacks. Just a sea of the same gray shirt, again and again, all topped by grinning faces. Everyone blurred together.

Finally, Foggy finished his speech, and everyone applauded and shouted and whistled. They were called up, table by table, to get dinner, with each kid taking a tray, just like the school lunch line. The food was much better, though: the pizza was real pizza, the apple didn't have any bruises, and the pudding was so good Parker wished she could go back for seconds. The rest of her cabin chatted and laughed while they ate, whispering about the upcoming campfire and the boys waving at them from across the hall, and Parker could only listen, trying to glean any clues about her cabinmates and the camp from what little she could hear. Jasmine and Maeve talked about their summer reading and gossiped about the other counselors, and Parker wanted to talk to them, as she was always good with adults and near-adults, but she suspected that sucking up would make her cabin hate her even more.

After the kids put up their trays, they ran outside like it was the last day of school, all headed toward the same trail into the forest. Parker stayed with Maeve and Jasmine, hanging back a bit, hoping to find someone, anyone, who was likewise getting their feet wet for the first time. But all the other kids were gone, and soon even the counselors took off jogging, forcing Parker to follow them on the hard-packed dirt path winding among tall, swaying trees as dusk slid into evening.

Earlier, Parker had noticed this path through the woods, veering off to the right of the lake. It led to a big clearing where all the trees had been removed in what seemed like a perfect circle. In the center was a big stone-lined pit full of logs and branches, all piled into a tidy cone, surrounded by concentric rings of long wooden benches. Each set of counselors went to opposite ends of a bench, and their rowdy campers lined up like ducklings between them. Again Parker found herself smooshed up against Jasmine.

She turned to the girl on her other side and said, "Hi, I'm Parker. What's your name?"

The girl looked as if she thought Parker might be contagious, but she glanced nervously at Jasmine and said, "Kaylee." Then she quickly turned back to the girl next to her and began whispering furiously.

Parker deflated a little. She was used to this kind of treatment back home, after the Ice Cream Incident, but every dream she'd had of reinventing herself at camp shriveled up and died in that moment. Cassandra had set her up for failure, she just knew it. Cassandra must've told them all about Parker's drawings and poetry, because even if this wasn't exactly bullying, it definitely wasn't the "friends for life" Camp Care had promised.

Foggy and a couple of counselors were fussing with the firepit, and eventually the flames began to grow, seemingly right as night fell. The perky woman from the lake stood in front of the fire, leading everyone in a song about Camp Care, then some counselors did a skit about last year's prank war. They sang another song, there were more skits, and all the kids in the audience laughed like it was the funniest thing ever— except Parker. She didn't know any of the songs, she didn't get any of the skits or inside jokes or know any of the characters involved or their nicknames. Whatever Pancake Night was, the Camp Care kids were apparently bonkers for it.

"Don't worry," Jasmine said, nudging her shoulder. "You'll know every word by Wednesday, and next year, all the skits will make sense."

Parker didn't tell her that the songs were stupid and she wouldn't be here next year unless she got bullied again and the school board needed to bribe her. She mostly just felt weird and unlikeable and sorry for herself. When her cabin got up to join the line for s'mores, she followed like a zombie. Even other kids couldn't ruin s'mores, right?

She wasn't paying attention, and in the jumble of kids hungry for chocolate or sneakily claiming a second s'mores packet, she got shifted away from her cabin. If they'd been nice at all, she would've fought her way back to them, but it was almost a relief, being unnoticed between two other cabins who didn't know who she was. All the boys on her left were talking about who would win some capture the flag tournament called Flag Wars, and the girls on her right were alternately giggling about the boys and bemoaning the way the boys never let them go for the flag.

Someone put two graham crackers in her hands, and someone else gave her half a chocolate bar, and then Foggy slid a hot marshmallow off a long stick and onto her crackers, his grin dancing in the firelight.

"See? I told you you'd settle in fine!" he said, and it was just too much.

Parker stepped away from the crackling fire and the laughing kids, scuttling to the back row of benches and sitting down

in a shadow where she hoped no one would notice her. She
lined up her graham crackers and chocolate and smooshed
down her marshmallow, taking a big bite and burning the roof
of her mouth.

Movement caught her eye—a subtle shifting on the other
side of the fire, in the shadows under the trees. It was another
girl sitting alone, like Parker, but the other girl didn't have a
s'more in her hands. She had dozens of bracelets on each wrist,
friendship bracelets and jelly bracelets stacked almost to her
elbows, and she fiddled with them nervously. Her long blond
hair tumbled messily over her face, but somehow Parker could
tell she was sad. Parker finished her s'more, dusted off her
hands, and purposefully marched around the periphery of the
benches, heart lifting with the hope that there might be one
person in this crazy camp who felt as lonely as she did.

"Parker!"

Her head snapped up, and Maeve waved from the Possum
cabin bench.

"Come on, you need to learn the Possum cheer!"

Parker looked back to the girl under the trees, but she was
gone. She scanned the benches but couldn't spot her. Then
again, the whole campfire area was a riot of flame and shadow,
every kid wearing the exact same thing. It was almost impossible to track anyone. She frowned, hoping she would catch sight
of the girl again during daylight, when Maeve wasn't yelling
and waving, calling even more attention to the one weirdo who
didn't fit in.

Well, maybe one weirdo . . . out of two.

Parker returned to her bench, annoyed but hopeful, and forced herself to focus on the Possum cabin cheer, which was just as embarrassing as it sounded, with a funny little dance at the end. It surprised her that Cassandra DiVecchio was willing to throw herself into Camp Care, doing things that KJ and Olivia would use to destroy her if they had proof back home. The lack of phones and cameras here apparently changed the rules. Cassandra had probably told them she was in Paris or Las Vegas or something fancy. If Parker had a phone, she would definitely take pictures of Cassandra doing the possum dance—

No.

No, she wouldn't be like them. Cassandra deserved the same freedom to be a dork as anyone else. Even if she was still somehow ruining Parker's life four hours from home, that didn't mean Parker was the kind of person who would use that same power for evil.

Even if they had to make possum faces at the end of the cheer and wiggle around, making chittering noises.

After each cabin did its cheer—each one as ridiculous and embarrassing as the next—the counselors led the kids back down the dark path using giant flashlights. Parker had never been in the woods at night before—she'd never even been camping before—and the combination of dark stillness and furtive rustling set her hair on end. For the first time, it sunk in that she would be sleeping out here, practically outside, miles from civilization and hundreds of miles from her parents. She'd never been invited to a slumber party, which meant that her only experiences not sleeping in her own house or in a hotel with her parents involved her grandparents and their over-protective Chihuahua, Pudgy.

"Does the cabin door lock?" she quietly asked Jasmine, hoping she didn't sound scared.

"There aren't any bears, so you don't need to worry!" Maeve answered too loudly, which made Parker cringe. That wasn't what she'd asked, but her cabinmates were whispering furiously behind her. She heard "Oh my God, of course she would ask that," but she didn't know exactly what that meant, as it seemed like a perfectly reasonable question for people who knew slasher films existed.

The cabins, as it turned out, each had a front porch light and a screen door, and as they filed inside Possum cabin, Parker noted that the door did have a lock, though not a very complicated or sturdy one. It definitely wouldn't stop a bear or a serial killer with a machete—nor would the open windows, which were protected only by their screens. She was the last to enter the cabin, and the screen door slammed behind her, making everyone jump.

"Don't slam the screen door," Addison said.

"Sorry. I didn't mean to."

Multiple pairs of eyes rolled, and Parker hurried to her bunk to escape their stares. Maeve and Jasmine were both outside chatting with other counselors, but she didn't want to look bad for asking them too many questions, although she had many. She wasn't sure what happened next, if everyone just changed out in the open or what, so she pretended to dig through her bag while she watched to see what everyone else would do. The other girls pulled pajamas and toiletry kits out of their drawers, all looking to each other as if waiting for a silent signal. Parker dug out her pajamas and the gallon freezer bag that held her own toiletries and waited.

"Hey, where's my necklace?" Addison said, her voice so loud that everyone froze and stared at her.

"The one with the star?" Kaylee asked.

"Yeah, I always put it in my bag when we go to the lake so it won't get ruined. It's real gold."

Several of the girls hurried over to Addison's bunk. One checked under it while another looked behind her dresser. The rest of the girls crowded around, murmuring uneasily.

"She always wears that necklace," one said, a nervous girl with a thick honey-colored braid and glasses and a name tag that said HANNA.

"It's probably just in the bottom of her bag," a pretty Asian girl with a pixie cut added. Her name tag said CHARLOTTE.

Addison dumped out her bag, sending neatly folded clothes all over her bed. She grew more frantic as she pawed through her things, unfolding everything and checking all the bag's pockets.

"It's not here! My mom is going to freak out!" Having only seen Addison cool as a cucumber until now, Parker found it odd to see her so upset, face red and on the verge of tears. The necklace must've meant a lot to her.

"Maybe it fell between the floorboards?" Parker offered.

"Maybe," Addison said, nibbling her lip. "But I don't think so. I guess we could get Maeve's flashlight and look for a flash of metal."

"But nobody's going in the crawl space tonight." Hanna gave a little shiver. "Too creepy. Are you sure you didn't leave it in the bathroom?"

"No," Addison said with a definitive headshake. "I remember taking it off and putting it in my toiletry bag. And it's not there anymore."

"Maybe somebody took it," Sydney said.

Much to Parker's surprise and horror, everyone stared at her.

"Why are you guys looking at me?" she asked, taking a step backward. Their collective glares felt like a physical blow.

Addison looked angry now. "Because we've all been best friends since we were in kindergarten, and you're the only new person. And—"

"So check her stuff," Cassandra interrupted. "And then we'll know."

Parker's jaw dropped, but she quickly recovered her speech. "Yeah, sure. I didn't take anything, so feel free to go through my bags and dresser. Whatever."

Everyone exchanged suspicious glances. Parker stared at

the door, hoping Maeve or Jasmine would come in and put a stop to this—this inquisition. Even though she knew she'd done nothing wrong, she started to feel guilty, like she was in trouble. It hurt that these girls just assumed she was terrible. Addison gingerly opened the top drawer of Parker's dresser, frowning as if she didn't really want to do it but had no choice, while Sydney pointed at Parker's backpack and said, "Open it."

Parker was reaching for her pack when Addison shouted, "Here it is!"

As she pulled a gold necklace out of Parker's dresser, everyone stared, first at the necklace and then at Parker.

"I didn't take that!" Parker gasped. "I swear! I've never even seen it before!"

"Then why's it in your dresser?" Sydney asked. "Did it just appear there by magic?"

Parker's whole body was shaking, her throat gone bone-dry and her breath coming fast, like she was in one of those nightmares where you can't breathe. "I don't know why it's there! I haven't even been in the cabin since I left for the lake."

Addison looked at her with so much hurt in her eyes, the necklace clenched in her fist. "I was the only one who wanted to trust you." She shook her head. "I was obviously wrong."

"Hey, this is my diary!" Kaylee called as she stood over Parker's open drawer. "And Hanna, this is your lucky scrunchie!"

Parker stared into her top dresser drawer. In addition to the sky-blue diary, there was a ratty old velvet scrunchie, a small stuffed rabbit, and a miniature unicorn—things she definitely hadn't seen before, much less taken.

"Oh my god! You *are* a klepto!" a tall girl with deep brown skin and intricate braids—Zoe—howled as she claimed her unicorn and cradled it against her chest.

"Freak," Hanna muttered as she snatched back the scrunchie and tossed the stuffed rabbit to Sydney.

"I swear—I'll swear on anything—I've never seen those things before. I didn't take them!" Parker protested. It felt like she was being backed into a corner against her will, and every time she met someone's eyes, hoping to find pity, she found only disgust or hate.

"It doesn't matter what you say," Addison said. "That's our stuff."

"But how would I know if a scrunchie was lucky?" Parker said. "I've never even met you before. It just looks ratty and old."

Hanna sneered. "I'm not the one who has to answer questions."

Addison glanced at the door. "Should we tell the counselors?"

"Please, no—" Parker started. It wasn't like she was having a particularly nice time at camp, but that didn't mean she wanted to be sent home on the first night in disgrace.

"We shouldn't," Cassandra said, stepping forward nervously. "Like, if she does it again, then we will. So she shouldn't do it again." She raised her eyebrows at Parker. "But, Parker, you should definitely stop trying to hang with us. I don't want to hang with a klepto."

"I'm not a klepto. I've never stolen anything in my life!" Parker shouted.

The girls all turned away, shaking their heads.

"That's exactly what a thief would say," someone muttered.

Parker could only stand there, utterly ashamed and confused even though she'd done nothing wrong. The other girls picked up their pajamas and toiletries but kept glancing back at their bunks as if they didn't trust Parker not to steal their underwear.

"You guys, I have my locking travel case," Sydney said. "You can put your valuables in here for the week." She threw Parker a disgusted glance and clicked open a silver box. The scrunchie, diary, rabbit, and unicorn went in there, but Addison had put her necklace back on and was clutching it to her chest like she might never take it off again.

When the girls had filed off to the bathroom, Parker slammed her face into her pillow just in time to catch the hot tears that came pouring out.

She'd dreamed of making friends here, of finally fitting in. But again she was on the outside, and not just because she was weird—but because everyone was convinced she was a thief. There was nothing she could do to prove otherwise, other than try to catch the real thief in the act. But why would one of the group steal from the rest? She pulled away from her pillow, dashing away her tears.

It had to be Cassandra. Cassandra had set her up somehow.

Cassandra knew Addison's necklace was important. She knew which scrunchie, out of all the ratty scrunchies in the world, was lucky.

And she had already proven that she was willing to embarrass Parker.

She had to think of some way to expose what Cassandra had done.

The girls returned from the bathroom, and Maeve and Jasmine came inside, joking around. Judging by their easygoing moods, they had no idea what had just transpired. Picking up her pajamas and toiletries, Parker hurried outside, careful not to let the screen door slam again. The woods were quiet—she must've been one of the last ones making this trip. She followed the glowing orange overhead lights, hurrying through the shadowy splotches between their warmth. When she reached the bathroom, the lights were off. Somewhere inside, something dripped. Even though it was a warm night, it seemed colder near the bathroom, dark and wet like a basement.

Before stepping inside, Parker felt along the wall until she discovered the light switch. Why would anyone even turn it off? The fluorescents buzzed to life, flickering as they illuminated the dripping sinks and wet floors bedecked with bits of toilet paper and a single fallen Q-tip. There was a breeze from the open windows, making the plastic shower curtains eerily sway, and the light over the last toilet stall flickered and flashed brightly before going dark.

Just moments ago, this bathroom would've been crowded with girls, each jockeying for a toilet or shower stall to change in, chattering and laughing and knocking toiletry bags off the sinks. But now the building felt unwelcoming, cold, coiled like a snake. Parker trotted into the first toilet stall and hurriedly pulled out her pajamas. It was tricky changing in her sneakers, and she made a note to wear her flip-flops the next time she came here. As she slipped her new Camp Care shirt off over her head, she got tangled for a moment and had to fight her way out. It was a stupid, scratchy, ugly shirt, the same one they'd had since the 1950s, and she had been saving her new clothes just for camp and now wouldn't even get to wear them.

The whole situation was just so *horrible*.

Everything about this camp had been designed to make people equal, so why was she still coming in last? She threw the Camp Care shirt on the floor and furiously kicked it outside the stall and put her head against the door as the tears sprung up again. She hated it here, hated the hot, wet air and the boring uniforms and the way everyone knew everything except her. She hated that there was nothing she could study, no rule book she could read, no teacher to ask for the information that would lead her to success. She hated that everyone knew everyone else and that Cassandra's rumors would spread beyond her own cabin to all the girls and boys and even counselors, probably.

She didn't want to go back to the cabin. For now, as she let the tears come, she was glad to be alone.

Her sobs had fallen off to snuffles when footsteps thudded on the tile—someone else who needed the facilities. She cleared her throat and flushed the toilet, desperate to hide the sounds of her sorrow.

The footsteps were slow and squeaky, almost squelchy, like the other girl's sneakers were wet—and like she was a little nervous or shy. She walked a few steps and stopped, totally silent.

A hand reached down and offered Parker her shirt from under the door.

A hand attached to a wrist stacked with bracelets.

"Is this yours?"

The voice was soft, almost fearful, like she was scared to talk at all and dreading the possibility of unkindness. Parker knew how that felt.

She took the shirt, noting the bright, beautiful colors of the friendship bracelets. "Yeah, thanks." The hand withdrew, but the girl didn't step away. Parker could see her black Keds and folded white socks under the door. Red clay mud stained the rubber edges of her shoes. "I like your bracelets," Parker offered.

The girl's feet shuffled. "Oh. Wow. Thanks. I made a lot of them myself."

Parker was fully dressed, but she knew that if she stepped out of the stall, the girl would see her red, puffy, tearstained face, and things would get awkward. She wasn't ready to tell a stranger what had happened today, not when the stranger, like the girls of Possum cabin, might believe the rumor instead of Parker.

"That's really cool," she said. "I've always wanted to learn how to make friendship bracelets."

"They'll teach you here," the girl said, which wasn't quite the invitation Parker had hoped for. "Whenever your cabin does crafts. At least, they used to."

"I'm Parker Nelson."

"I'm Jenny McAllister."

Another awkward silence. Parker was good at filling those.

"Will I see you around? Maybe we can do crafts together? I think I saw you at the campfire tonight. It's my first year, and I don't know anything, and my cabin . . ." How to say it? "They don't get me. Like, at all. I just don't fit in."

A sad sigh. "I know that feeling," Jenny said. "I don't really fit in either. But cabins have to do all their activities together."

"Maybe we could sit together at the campfire tomorrow?"

The shoes shuffled. "I'll try." It was weird how Jenny seemed kind of sad about it when Parker was just super jazzed to maybe have someone to talk to who didn't think the worst of her.

"Excuse me—emergency!" a new voice called as flip-flops flapped on the tiles and a stall door slammed shut. Whatever the poor girl had eaten, Parker was really glad she hadn't had the same thing.

She stepped out of the stall, hoping maybe she and Jenny could talk outside, but Jenny was gone.

The only sign of her was a few light sneaker imprints of wet Georgia clay mud, rust red under the cool fluorescent lights.

When she went outside, there was no one there.

The other girl had disappeared.

7.

Parker hurried back to her cabin, but the mood inside was even more uncomfortable than a bathroom that reeked of lactose intolerance. The girls had been excitedly chattering, but the moment Parker closed the door, they went silent and stared at her briefly before each rolling away to show her their back. She clambered up onto her own bed and tried to get comfortable. Even if it had her sheets and pillow and blanket from home, it was nowhere close to cozy. The mattress was thin, and she could feel the slats through it. It rustled every time she moved, making her extra aware of how she must be bothering the counselor trying to sleep below her. She had no music or TV or book to lull her unconscious. Just a room full of softly breathing, silently seething girls who hated her. As her eyelids fluttered down, she thought she heard footsteps outside, crunching in the leaves, but . . . well, people had to use the bathroom, didn't they?

She must've fallen asleep at some point, as she woke up at

dawn, groggy and confused, to the sound of a poorly played trumpet piped in through creaky speakers. She rolled over—and almost fell out of the top bunk. Thank goodness it had railings. Around her, the other campers stirred and stretched and shuffled through their things, but Parker lay in her bunk, staring through the nearest cobweb-dusted screen window. It was a bright, pretty morning, but it was altogether too early to be awake in summer, and she wasn't looking forward to a day of activities with her cabin.

As soon as the other girls left for the bathroom in a big clot, she carefully climbed down from her bunk. Jasmine was sitting on her own mattress, glasses on and hair in a silky scarf as she looked through a sheaf of stapled papers.

"Hey, Jasmine, can I talk to you?" Parker started.

Jasmine put the papers down and turned to give Parker her full attention. "Of course. That's what counselors are here for."

Parker took a deep breath. "All the other girls think I stole their stuff, but I didn't. I was framed. And when I told them the truth, they didn't believe me."

Before Jasmine could respond, Maeve bounded over from across the cabin, French-braided pigtails bouncing. The frown sat oddly on her face, like it wasn't an expression she wore very often. "Yeah, I heard about that. The evidence doesn't look good."

Jasmine looked from Parker to Maeve, and Parker could tell the moment she took sides. "All the other girls in this cabin have been friends since they were little," Jasmine said, a story that was starting to get pretty old, in Parker's opinion. "And none of them has ever stolen anything from anybody."

"And there were stories . . ." Maeve looked at Parker and shook her head. "Cassie said that you have a reputation back at your old school. That you've had issues stealing things before."

"That's a lie! You can call my old school and ask. I've never had a single discipline problem. It has to be Cassandra setting me up. She's a mean girl back home, and she must've framed me—"

"Excuse me," Maeve said, all chipperness gone, replaced with frosty disdain. "But Cassie is my cousin, and there's no way she would do that."

Parker filed that away—and understood that she had now lost any chance at having Maeve believe her or help her. There had to be another argument . . .

"Okay, but—well, why would I want that stuff? A stranger's diary? Some scraped-up old figurine? A ratty scrunchie covered with ten years of someone else's dandruff? It's all useless to anyone who doesn't own it. And since I just got here, how would I even know what was special? And let's be honest—I'm a straight-A kid. If I was going to steal something, I wouldn't be stupid enough to leave it in my top drawer, where it would be found instantly. It's clearly a setup."

Jasmine threw Parker a pitying look. "Look, we have the word of nine girls we know and trust . . . and then we have you saying the complete opposite. Maeve and I didn't witness the incident, and nobody wants to take it up the chain of command. If it happens again, though, you'll have to meet with

Director Fogarty, so you just need to toe the line and accept that you're going to have to work hard to regain your cabin's trust."

"Luckily, you'll have plenty of chances to do that, as we've got tons of fun activities and team-building exercises!" Maeve's exclamation points were definitely back, although they now had a sarcastic, cutting edge. "So just focus on being the best friend you can be!"

Parker still had so many questions—most important, if she was allowed to sit with other cabins at the campfire and what kinds of activities they'd be doing—but she was beginning to see that the counselors weren't adults with authority. They were just slightly older teens who wanted to do as little work as possible and avoid dealing with uncomfortable situations.

"Will do," she said, giving an awkward salute. "Is it okay if I change in here?"

"Sure. We'll just face away," Jasmine said. She turned away. Maeve left, and Parker was grateful that at least she wouldn't have to fight for space in a crowded bathroom where her cabinmates would be looking for ways to alienate her. She crowded into the corner and changed the way they did for PE at school, which turned never being exposed into an art form.

By the time the other campers returned, she was in her Camp Care uniform, hair brushed and teeth . . . well, rubbed with toothpaste. Her dental health could suffer for one week. The other girls cavorted around Maeve as she led them out of the cabin, begging her to tell them what their first activity was, but she pretended to zip her mouth shut and skipped along with a silent smirk, taking them to Friendship Hall for a breakfast of cereal and fruit.

The first activity turned out to be rock climbing, which was actually pretty cool. They had to wear helmets and harnesses, but Parker couldn't believe the camp had a super-high wall. As the only new camper, Parker got pulled aside by one of the instructors, a pimply teen guy named Tim, and had to do a ton of listening and practice before they would let her on the real wall. She thought she would totally ace it, but . . . rock climbing was really hard. She could see the holds, and she wasn't scared, but soon her hands hurt and her legs were jelly. Some of the other girls could scamper up like squirrels, but a few, including Cassandra, weren't that great either. It was pretty fun seeing her fall on her butt.

As they stood on the ground, watching the more skilled girls climb ever higher, Parker sidled over to Cassandra.

"You did it, didn't you?" Parker whispered. "You spread lies and framed me."

Cassandra's eyes stared directly forward as she spoke softly so no one else would hear. "I don't know what you're talking about."

Red-hot rage fizzled through Parker's blood, and she had to force herself to whisper and not scream. "Yes, you do. It's just like back home. Why do you hate me so much?"

At that, Cassandra faced her and rolled her eyes. "I don't

hate you. You're just . . . ugh!" She shook her head and stomped over to talk to Maeve, and Parker just had to hope the conversation wasn't about her.

Soon a xylophone *bing*ed over the loudspeaker, and they all thanked Tim and gave him fist bumps before Maeve led them in another direction. All the other girls cheered when they saw the crafts cabin, and when the door opened, Parker understood why. The big airy room was absolutely stuffed with shelves and shelves of colorful art supplies, and the walls were covered with artwork. The pretty instructor, Bailey, wore cat's-eye glasses and looked like Ms. Frizzle, and Parker automatically loved her. Bailey pulled down a huge bucket of embroidery floss, and they worked on friendship bracelets, just as Jenny'd said they would. Parker struggled to learn the easiest one while the other girls forged ahead with wide, multicolored bracelets that looked a lot like the ones Jenny wore.

"Why is this so hard?" she grumbled.

"Because you've never done it before and you have no right to rock it," Bailey said, helping Parker untwist her bracelet. "They've been doing this since they were babies. Don't worry. You'll get the hang of it. You get to keep the clipboard and your baggie of floss, so you can make bracelets whenever you want."

Parker liked that, but she didn't like how all the other girls already had clipboards with their names painted on them, along with layers and layers of painted designs. Her own clipboard was plain brown wood, shiny and new. It just seemed like everything at Camp Care existed to make new people feel like outsiders, which seemed very much against the spirit of caring.

When the xylophone rang again and all the fist bumps had been distributed, Maeve took the girls back to the cabin to change into their swimsuits.

"I know it's bad timing," Maeve announced to everyone with a shrug. "Nobody wants to do the swim test right after lunch. So just eat light and I'll make sure to bring a snack for afterward."

This time Parker had to take her suit to the bathroom to change, but she hurried into one of the wet-floored shower stalls, as far away from the other girls as possible. She'd chosen a frilly suit, but all the other girls had plain ones that went with the general Camp Care aesthetic. She put her uniform over it, as the other girls did, and silently sat by Jasmine at lunch. The rock climbing had made her ravenous, and she loved chicken nuggets and fries, so at least it was comfort food.

Out at the lake, the other girls tossed off their uniforms, but instead of diving into the cool water, they politely lined up on the sand by the woman with the perky ponytail and Camp Care visor.

"You guys know the drill," she said with a grin.

"For most of you, it's just a formality." She blew her whistle. One by one, as she called their names, the other campers waded into the water, swam out to the end of the dock, treaded water as she timed them with her stopwatch, floated on their backs, and then swam back in. As each girl accomplished this task, the woman put a checkmark by her name. The girls were then free to swim on their own, and most of them chose to paddle out to the floating dock, where a tan lifeguard in red board shorts lounged on a bright-red chair, wearing sunglasses and tossing his bleached-blond hair.

Finally, her name got called—last, of course. "Parker Nelson, you're next. I'm Belinda, by the way, otherwise known as the lake activities director. Do you have any experience in the water?"

"Oh, definitely." Parker grinned. "I've taken loads of classes."

Feeling confident, she nodded to Belinda and waded into the lake. The water was cold but not horrible, and it felt delicious after a hot, sweaty morning of rock climbing. It was a little disturbing when the sandy ground fell out from beneath her feet, but she was decent enough at a front crawl, which is what the other girls had done. She plowed out toward the end of the dock, alone but happy, glad that finally she was doing an activity she didn't suck at. When she reached the end of the dock, she turned around to face Belinda and started treading water. She wasn't sure how long she had to paddle until Belinda blew her whistle, but it hadn't seemed very long when she'd watched the others from the shore.

Her arms were starting to get tired, but Parker could do this. When she looked down, she couldn't help noticing how very dark the water was. It was murky down to her waist and then completely opaque. When she glanced sideways under the dock, it was even darker, ink black. There were weird bulges under the dock, algae-covered chunks of Styrofoam and twisted metal wire. She thought she saw a shape moving underwater, and—

Something grabbed her ankle.

Parker jerked backward, mouth open, and gasped. As she desperately kicked to free her foot, her face slipped under the water, foul, muddy liquid gushing down her throat. She choked on it and spluttered, struggling to keep her head up. But whatever had her in its grip wouldn't let go. With no way to scream, all she could do was hold her breath and kick with both feet, pawing for air.

Dragged downward into the dark, she struggled to see what her foot was caught on, but the deeper she went, the darker the lake became. When she looked up, she could see the mossy green water and sunlight overhead, but she couldn't reach the surface.

When she was almost out of breath, strong hands grabbed her and pulled her up. She opened her mouth to suck in a big breath and spluttered as the good-looking teen lifeguard dragged her in. Every time she tried to speak, she could only cough. It didn't occur to her to be mortified until the tall, tanned boy in the red trunks was carrying her under her arms and legs like a little baby.

Once she was sitting on the sand, she gave in to coughing until she could take a solid breath.

"You okay?" the lifeguard asked.

The rest of the lake had gone silent, and when Parker looked up, everyone was staring at her.

"Something pulled me down," she said.

The lifeguard shook his head. He looked a little scared. "But are you okay? Are you hurt?"

"No. But I'm telling you—something grabbed my ankle and pulled me underwater."

Belinda squatted down, frowning. "Yeah, there's nothing in the lake that could do that. Kids'll say they've seen gators, but it's way too cold." She leaned in closer. "But—hey. It's okay. We can help you practice your skills, and you'll pass the test next year."

Parker's jaw fell open. "So you're saying that not only do you not believe that something grabbed me, but *I failed the swimming test?*"

Belinda's smile was pitying "When Jackson has to get his hair wet, you've definitely failed."

"But I swam out there! You watched me do it. I can tread water! I can float on my back!"

The lifeguard put a hand on Parker's shoulder and gave her a look that was equal parts doubtful and wry. "If you really, truly believe that something pulled you underwater, why would you want to swim out there again anyway?" He patted her shoulder and sauntered back down the dock.

"Either way, rules are rules," Belinda added. "No big deal. By the end of the week, we'll have you swimming like an otter with the rest of your cabin, I promise." It was clear that Belinda was infected with that same Camp Care attitude of unflagging cheerfulness combined with a total inability to see the truth. Parker's head hung; all of Possum cabin was staring at her from the floating dock as they witnessed her shame. There was no way they would let her swim with them, like an otter or no.

Belinda stood up to go talk to Maeve, but before she was gone, Parker noticed that her name on the clipboard had a big, ugly *X* beside it.

When she looked out to the dock in the middle of the lake, everyone in her cabin was whispering about her, as were the rest of the boys and girls. They were all dripping wet. Any one of them could've pulled her under as a joke. But why? And who?

Calling her a liar was one thing. Trying to drown her was another.

6.

At least no one made fun of Parker once it was time for their next activity. Most of her cabin looked worried as they followed Maeve back toward the bathroom so everyone could change.

"Are you sure you're okay?" Kaylee asked when Parker was hanging up her suit. "You looked like you were legit drowning."

Parker was glad for the attention but hated that it came in the form of pity. "Actually, drowning doesn't typically look like drowning. People who are drowning—they don't thrash and scream. Their heads just kind of bob, and then they can't stay afloat any longer." The girl gave her a weird look, so she added, "They made us watch videos at swim class."

After that, Kaylee shook her head and faded back in with the rest of the group. Being scared had apparently caused Parker to completely forget that she wasn't going to blabber at people anymore, and it made her feel like even more of an idiot. Maeve gave everyone bags of chips and led them down a trail Parker hadn't followed before. After they passed a blackened, burned, twisted tree, everyone except Parker groaned.

"What's going on?" she asked, hurrying to catch up with them.

"Hiking," Addison said grimly.

"What's wrong with hiking?"

"It's the worst of all the activities." Addison frowned as her hand strayed up to possessively clutch her necklace, and Parker decided she would rather hang back and have no idea what was going on than deal with further pity or distrust.

The groaning was definitely merited, Parker soon learned. Maeve dropped the girls off with a skinny, hyper guy named Terry, who took off at a pace that was practically speed walking. As they jogged to keep up with him, he pointed out the sorts of things Parker would've loved to learn more about— interesting plants, unusual rocks, creeks, birds' nests. But he walked and talked so fast that there was no time to stop and really investigate anything, and he didn't slow down for questions at all. Most of the girls were huffing and puffing.

Parker was pretty sure she could now find her way from Possum cabin to Friendship Hall to the lake, but the rest of the trails were tangled up in her memory like spaghetti, and she soon had no idea where they might be in relation to the rest of the camp. There should've been signs or a map, but when everyone else already knew everything, apparently no one thought that was necessary. Parker wondered how old kids had to be to run around without supervision, as she'd already noticed that the youngest kids had three counselors to a cabin and were constantly being led around holding a knotted rope, all in a line like baby ducks. After a few years here, the kids had Camp Care in their veins and could probably find their way around campus on a moonless night. The jerks.

"What's that?" she asked as something gleamed under the forest canopy.

She pointed, and Terry glanced over his shoulder and grimaced.

"Nothing. Just some old junk, probably."

Parker wasn't willing to slow down and get left behind out here, but she was pretty sure what she'd seen was the big fence Addison had warned her about, topped with shiny razor wire. It was soon lost in the undergrowth as they marched on, and she had to assume it marked off someone else's land or maybe one of those places where people hunted deer. She knew there was plenty of that up here, in north Georgia, although her mother had assured her that June was not hunting season.

By the end of the hike, she was super exhausted and hadn't learned much except that there were tons of cool things out here in the woods if only she could have slowed down enough to appreciate them. Maeve was reading an old paperback as she waited for them on a log, and everyone's grumbly mood vastly improved as she led them back to their cabin to chill for half an hour before dinner. Parker hadn't brought any technology—because she wasn't allowed to—but she hadn't brought any books either. Having never been to camp, she didn't know there would be any down time, although now that she was here, it seemed perfectly obvious. Every other girl pulled out a book—the same new, hardback YA, like they were a book club. Parker was the only one without something to read, and she hated how it made her feel like she was the dumbest one when in fact she'd probably read more books than any of them.

"Do you have any more books?" she asked Maeve.

Maeve looked up from her battered paperback. "I mean, you can just go to the library."

"There's a library?"

Maeve caught herself before she could roll her eyes, and for a moment there, Parker could definitely tell she was related to Cassandra. "It's just a little free library made from an old stump. It's on the other side of Friendship Hall, near the boys' cabins. You can't miss it."

"And I can just . . . go there?"

This time, Maeve did the full eye roll—clearly her exclamation points couldn't last long against someone like Parker. "Of course. You're not five!"

Parker could feel everyone in the room listening in, even if they were hiding behind their identical books. She was more than glad to have a reason to leave for a while, so she hurried out and followed the path to the staggered line of cabins on the other side of the main hall. She hadn't been over here before, and to be honest, she hadn't really given it much thought. This side was all boys, and even if the girls of her cabin got giggly around them, Parker wasn't interested anymore—not after that embarrassing incident at the lake. She kept an eye out for Jenny on her way over, but she didn't see her anywhere.

Now that she was here, she noticed the subtle differences in how the cabins were placed. Some boys were playing Frisbee, others were playing hacky sack, but no one was paying any attention to her, which was a nice change from the constant scrutiny of her own cabin.

Maeve was right: she couldn't miss it. The library was eight feet tall, a dead, hollowed-out tree with shelves hewn inside and a glass-paned door firmly fitted across the front. There was nothing as nice and new as the popular book her cabinmates were reading, but there was a lot more variety than she would've expected from a stump.

She picked up a book she recognized and liked from when she was younger, but then she put it down. She had to walk back into her cabin with something sophisticated under her arm so the other girls would know she was smart and a reader who didn't shy away from big books. She almost picked up a horror book, but she chickened out. She was still far too aware that nothing but a few flimsy screens stood between her and the forest at night. She settled for a big YA fantasy she'd heard of but never read, something about fairies, and made sure to turn the handle so the door would stay firmly shut and the books had no chance of getting ruined by the weather.

Back in the cabin, Parker settled down in her bunk and started reading. Every time she glanced around the room, she saw the same dang book. It made her so mad that it was hard to concentrate. She couldn't help wondering if every new person felt this way, or if maybe there were cabins where the kids got all mixed up each year and thought newcomers were actually fun. She was so distracted that she barely made it through three pages before the dinner bell rang.

The other girls stowed their books and headed for dinner, leaving Parker to follow more slowly. There was no reason to rush—everyone got the same food, and it's not as if she was hurrying to get a good seat. She sat in the same place she always sat: with her cabin, on the other side of a counselor.

Dinner was spaghetti with the good kind of garlic roll, and as Parker nibbled, she scanned the cafeteria for Jenny, or anyone, really, who looked interesting. Since everyone wore the same uniform, no one really caught her eye, although some of the boys from Groundhog cabin were throwing grapes at Cassandra's end of the table, trying to get the other girls' attention. She didn't see Jenny, but she did see a few kids get up and leave.

"Are we allowed to eat outside?" she asked Jasmine.

Jasmine didn't even look up from her book. "You can go outside, but you can't take your tray out there. Litter has to get put away, or Foggy gets really upset. Some kids spend all their free time in the craft cabin or fishing or whatever. But we do a head count at the campfire, so whenever you hear the xylophone, you need to make sure you hurry." She looked up, her eyes showing . . . yet more pity. Big surprise. "If you don't show up, everyone has to go to Friendship Hall, and all the counselors have to come looking for you, and it can get embarrassing."

Parker nodded. She definitely didn't want to be further embarrassed.

"And maybe don't be in our cabin alone," Jasmine warned with an awkward, almost apologetic grimace.

Face burning, Parker dumped her tray and headed out to the craft cabin. There were two other people there, one kid drawing manga characters in a sketchbook and the other working on a small loom. They looked up at Parker as she entered but said nothing. She didn't know if this was because they'd witnessed the lake incident or because they were just concentrating, so she gave a little wave and found her clipboard on the Possum cabin shelf. Sitting down by the window, she applied herself to her friendship bracelet, determined to finish it before the sun set and it was campfire time.

It was calming, focusing on the smooth, colorful thread as the sky outside went pink and then purple. It was so nice having calm and quiet, not being stared at and whispered about. Making the friendship bracelet forced her to think just hard enough that her brain couldn't remind her what had happened at the lake, how scary it had been, and how awful it felt afterward when no one had believed her. She was getting the rhythm of the string, loop and through and pull and tighten, loop and through and pull and tighten. It wasn't a perfect bracelet, but it changed colors three times and was long enough to go around her wrist. When the xylophone *bing*ed, she tied a knot and snipped the strings before following the other kids out to the campfire clearing.

At least she knew what to expect now. She found her cabin in their usual place and checked in with Jasmine, who handed her a bottle of bug spray. As she sat on the end of the bench, she excitedly scanned the crowd for Jenny. She finally spotted her sitting behind all the benches, on the ground under the trees, fiddling with the bracelets on her wrists.

"I'm going to go talk to a friend," she told Jasmine, and Jasmine nodded and watched her go.

Jenny looked up as she got near but didn't stand, so Parker flopped down beside her in the grass. It had been mown recently and was tickly but not prickly.

"How was your day?" she asked, since Jenny hadn't looked up yet and seemed kind of sad.

"The same as always."

"I brought you something. Here."

Parker held out the friendship bracelet she'd just finished. When Jenny didn't immediately take it, she felt awkward. "I just learned how to make them today. I know it's not as fancy as your other ones, definitely not as pretty, but you're literally the only person who's been nice to me at all, so I thought— I mean, you don't have to—"

Gently, reverently, Jenny took the bracelet and expertly tied it on her right wrist, nearest her hand.

"It's really nice," she said. "Nobody's ever given me one before."

"But you have so many—"

"I made them all."

There had to be dozens, some old and some new, some thin and some thick, some shiny and some ragged, all layered with jelly bracelets.

"They're beautiful," Parker said. "Really."

Jenny reached for a particularly nice one in various shades of pink, shiny new with a fancy arrow pattern. She took it off and reached over to tie it onto Parker's empty wrist.

"Does this mean we're friends now?" Jenny asked.

"I hope so. It would be so cool to have someone at this stupid camp who didn't hate me."

Jenny snorted. "Yeah, tell me about it."

Down below, Director Fogarty finally had the campfire going. "Does it always take him this long to start a fire?" Parker said.

Jenny chuckled. "Yeah, it always takes them forever. You think they'd just throw a can of gas on it and save everyone the time, but that's not the Camp Care way."

They both laughed at that, and someone on the nearest bench turned around to stare. It felt good, being stared at for such a simple reason, for just laughing at an odd time with a friend. In response, Parker laughed louder. Everyone started singing the Camp Care song, and Jenny sang under her breath. Her voice was a little off-key, but she got most of the words right. Parker was comfortable enough to sing the chorus, at least, although she didn't have a lot of faith in her voice either. It felt nice, sitting next to someone, badly singing along with someone. She was glad she'd made the bracelet and given it to Jenny.

She plucked at the new bracelet on her wrist, turning it over to admire the arrow designs. "Could you teach me how to make this kind?" she asked.

Jenny's mouth twisted. "I don't know. It's hard to get away during the day."

Parker sighed and nodded. "I know what you mean. The counselors really keep us busy and crammed together. But I found the library today."

At that, Jenny perked up. "There's a library?"

Oh, the joy of being in the know!

"Yeah, it's on the far side of Friendship Hall from our cabins, on the boys' side. It's like a little free library, but in a big dead tree. You can't miss it."

"I've never seen it," Jenny said, looking down at the campfire. "I love reading."

"Me too! Do you like poetry?"

Jenny lit up. "I love Shel Silverstein. He just . . . gets it. How the world doesn't really make sense."

"Right?" Parker lit up, too. She'd never met anyone else who really liked poetry—or who would admit it publicly. "I think 'Put Something In' is my favorite, or maybe 'The Poet Tree.' I still remember when my second-grade teacher started reading his books and poems to us, and I thought the sidewalk actually had an end."

"It made me want to dance the first time I read it," Jenny admitted. "A loony-goony dance. I used to try to write poetry, but it's harder than it looks."

After the Ice Cream Incident, Parker definitely agreed. She wasn't ready to tell Jenny about that yet, though. "What's your favorite book series?"

"Maybe Baby-Sitters Club." Jenny turned the bracelets on her wrist back and forth. "I used to think about what it would be like to be friends with Claudia. She just seems so cool."

Parker was smiling so big her face hurt. "Me too! I love her style." She tugged at the hem of her Camp Care shirt. "I mean, any style is better than no style, right? How did you get your shirt knotted so well?"

Jenny looked down at her own shirt as if she'd forgotten she was wearing it. It was a little oversized, big enough to cuff the sleeves, and the fabric was softly worn Parker had to assume that after kids had been coming here for years, they would pride themselves on possessing shirts that showed their age, with stains from all their adventures.

"Oh, you just use a rubber band." Jenny slid one off her wrist from where it nestled among the bracelets and reached for Parker's shirt. It was kind of weird, but Parker let her, and soon her own shirt had a knot in it, too.

"Thanks!" she said. "I feel cooler already."

To her surprise, Jenny gave her a distrustful look. "Are you messing with me?"

"Definitely not. I'm . . ."

She paused. Even if they were surrounded by hundreds of other kids, it's like they were in their own little bubble.

"I'm not cool where I come from. Or in my cabin. I brought all new clothes, and I can't even wear them. I had to buy new uniforms, and they're so stiff and scratchy. Everyone in my cabin thinks I'm a klepto who can't swim, and I hate it."

Sympathy flashed in Jenny's dark eyes. "Why do they think you're a klepto?"

"Because someone framed me. Stole personal stuff from the other girls and stuck it in my top drawer. I think it was this girl from my school—Cassandra. The main reason I'm here is because she and her friends bullied me back home. She's a total mean girl. I hate her."

The campfire flickered in Jenny's dark eyes as she looked across all the kids on the benches and focused in on Possum cabin. "Ugh. Cassandra," she murmured.

Everyone else stopped singing and stood, signaling the time for s'mores. Parker jumped to her feet.

"Yes! S'mores! I didn't eat all my dinner. I'm starving."

But when she looked to Jenny, the other girl was still sitting down, arms hugging her knees.

"Aren't you coming down for s'mores?" she asked.

Jenny shook her head. "I . . . hate crowds. But I'll see you tomorrow night, right?"

"Definitely! Thanks again for the bracelet. I love it."

"I love mine, too."

Jenny stood and held out her pinkie. Grinning, Parker hooked her own pinkie around it.

"Best friends!" Jenny said.

"Sure!"

But Jenny paused, their fingers still linked. Her brow drew down. "You have to say it."

Parker felt a little weird calling someone she'd talked to for a total of twenty minutes her bestie, but she didn't want to go back to being alone or give up the bracelet, so she said, "Oh, yeah! Of course! Best friends!"

Jenny smiled at her, nodded once, and sat back down. Parker, who didn't mind crowds at all, got in line feeling happier than she had all day.

When she returned to the Possum cabin bench with her s'mores, no one paid her any attention at all. She looked for Jenny, but the shadows where they'd been sitting were too dark to see much now. Every so often, she ran her fingers over her new friendship bracelet.

It felt nice, finally having a friend.

7.

Now that Parker wasn't trying to fit in, her cabin mostly ignored her. It was as if she wasn't even there. She managed to change into her pajamas and finally brush her teeth, and then she was back in her bunk, realizing how exhausting today's rock climbing and hiking—and nearly drowning—had been. She was so tired that she fell asleep almost immediately and was soon waking up to the decidedly undulcet tunes of a poorly played trumpet.

It was like an instant replay of the day before, except that heavy clouds covered the sky. On the way to breakfast, the other girls begged and cajoled, but Maeve still wouldn't tell them their activities schedule. Jasmine left after breakfast again—she must've been assigned to run one of the activities while Maeve led the cabin around. Parker had on her new friendship bracelet and had done a decent enough job of knotting her tee like Jenny had. Cassandra saw the knot and raised her eyebrow but chose not to say anything. That was so Cassandra—she knew bullying wasn't allowed here, but she still found a way to make Parker feel less-than.

Parker of course had no idea where they were headed, as most of the trails still seemed like a wretched tangle, but all the other girls broke out in excited cheers as Maeve turned right down a path Parker was certain she hadn't seen before. The smell hit her first, but then she saw the barn waiting out beyond the forest, where the trees were cleared out in a verdant valley. Horses watched them from big pastures on either side of the wide dirt track, swishing their tails as they munched on grass. Parker had never taken horseback riding lessons, and she was really excited but also a little nervous. Everyone else here had surely been riding every summer for years, but she'd only ever sat on a pony at the local fair while someone else walked it around in boring circles.

The girls were quiet as they approached, and Parker as usual hung back a bit. A mom-aged woman met them just outside the barn, along with two teens who had to be twins, although they weren't perfectly identical. Her cabinmates took turns hugging each of them, and Parker sidled over to stand next to Maeve.

"A new girl!" the woman said. "Ever been on a horse before?"

Everyone turned to stare at Parker. She hated not knowing things. "Not really."

The woman smiled. "Excellent. I never get to teach any of these kids anything they don't already know. And old Gusty needs the exercise."

The rest of Possum cabin went into the barn with the twins, and all came out holding rope halters, but the woman—Beth—walked Parker through everything in a way that didn't make her feel stupid at all. Gusty was their old, dependable lesson horse, and when Parker met him in the field and offered him a dirty piece of carrot, he snuffled politely into her hand and gazed at her with eyes like melted chocolate, fringed in long white lashes. With Beth's help, she was able to bring Gusty into the barn, brush him, saddle him, and mount up at the same time as the other girls, so it wasn't too embarrassing. The saddle rubbed her bare legs, and the helmet felt a little loose, but she could make do. As long as she didn't fail at horseback riding as spectacularly as she'd failed her swim test, it would be fine.

They practiced riding around a fenced-in ring first, and Beth was right about Gusty—he just plodded along, following the other horses at a tortoise's pace. Parker couldn't help doing a million things wrong—Beth had told her to keep her heels down and her thumbs up and her gaze between Gusty's droopy ears, and it was just a lot to keep in mind while five feet off the ground. The other girls kept passing her like she was a grandma daring to use the fast lane. There were brown horses and black horses and a pretty spotted gray one, and Parker got to see each of them up close as they trotted around her again and again. She would've really liked horseback riding, probably, if she'd been wearing jeans and had been with literally anyone else in the entire world other than Cassandra and her groupies.

When Beth was satisfied that everyone could go, stop, turn around, and trot, she mounted her paint horse and the girls followed her out of the ring and toward a trail that led into the trees behind the barn. Parker and Gusty were supposed to be last, with one of the twins on her shiny golden horse taking up the rear.

"Don't worry if they leave us behind," the twin said. "We can go at your pace."

"What if I want to catch up?" Parker asked, not wanting to lag behind and become the subject of yet more gossip.

The twin laughed. "Then you can try to get Gusty to trot, but as you've already seen, he's pretty lazy until he wants something."

It was cooler under the trees, and even if plodding around the ring had been pretty annoying, the actual trail ride was fantastic. On yesterday's hike, Terry had dominated the forest sounds with his constant monologue, but here it was just the clop of hooves, the soft snuffle of horse noses, the trill of birdsong, and the rustling of endless bright green leaves. Every now and then, she heard something moving in the woods, somewhere nearby in the tangle of underbrush where she couldn't see it. A deer, maybe. Whatever it was, it definitely sounded bigger than a bird or squirrel, and Parker had the strange thought that it might be following them. She squinted into the shadows, hoping to see her first wild deer, but the forest beyond the trail was a shadowy, impenetrable place. As if it could sense her curiosity, whatever it was went silent, and she didn't hear the footsteps again.

Her cabinmates were quieter than usual, enjoying this special time, and after a few minutes, they were far ahead of her. Parker took a big breath and let it out in a whoosh, relaxing. For now, she wasn't anxious, she wasn't thinking about other people or what her hair and clothes were doing wrong. She couldn't even see the twin behind her, so it just felt like her and Gusty, chilling out. Maybe she would ask her mom about taking some horseback riding lessons when she got home—but on a horse with more gears than "slump."

Time went kind of funny—but then again, it seemed to do that when you weren't constantly checking the clock at school or the time on your phone. Parker was kind of zoned out, but when they hooked left down a new trail, Gusty went stiff under her and snorted, bringing her back to herself. She could feel the horse's energy change, his body tightening and his ears pricking up. His skin shuddered as he raised his head and gave a shrill whinny.

"Uh, what's he doing?" she asked nervously.

"He can be a little barn sour," the twin said behind her, clearly bored out of her mind. "He can tell when we're near home, and he wants to get there faster."

If Gusty had seemed sleepy and lazy before, now he was very much awake, and Parker became extremely aware that she was sitting on top of a thousand pounds of motivated beast. Gusty picked up his pace, and Parker struggled to keep her balance and tried to post as his plodding walk became a juddering trot.

"Just tighten up the reins and hold on," the twin called behind her. "If you sit down and tell him to whoa, he might chill a little."

Or he might not, Parker thought, pretty sure there was no way she could just sit down and say *whoa* while trying not to fall off. When Gusty jumped over a big root, her rear left the saddle for a moment, and she flung her arms around his neck like they'd practiced in the ring. Luckily, she got settled again and didn't have to do an emergency dismount, which would've been mortifying, even if the rest of her cabin wasn't right there to see it.

They went around a group of big bushes, and for the first time in a while, Parker finally saw the rump of the horse in front of her.

That rump was coming up a lot faster than she would've preferred.

"Whoa!" she said, pulling back on the reins and feeling guilty for hurting the horse's mouth. "Stop!"

But Gusty didn't stop. He plowed onward, his chest ramming into the horse in front of him. That horse took offense at having her butt bumped and jumped forward, annoying the horse in front of her. Soon several of the horses up front got sick of the melee behind them and squealed before taking off at a canter. The rest of the horses thought that was a great idea, apparently, including Gusty.

Parker grabbed the saddle horn and held on for dear life. Her reins flapped out of her other hand as the horses broke out of the forest and raced for the barn. The other girls were laughing and whooping like this was totally normal, but Parker was frozen in terror, unable to control the flopping of her legs or the direction of her horse. When Gusty finally slid to a stop, she hugged his neck and rolled off in the emergency dismount, glad to be back on the ground.

Parker could barely breathe, her feet were numb, and her heart was pounding like crazy. She grabbed for Gusty's reins to make sure he didn't do anything else mortifying, but he was back in tortoise mode, head hanging, ears drooping, as if he'd never run a day in his life.

"You need to learn to control your horse!" Cassandra said from somewhere overhead, still on her own mount, a beautiful red-brown horse with blue eyes and white legs. She looked like a queen, confident and tall. And mean.

"I'd love to!" Parker shot back. "But I currently have two hours of horse experience, and nobody told me he was secretly a dang racehorse!"

The other girls watched from atop their horses. Beth was on the ground, softly berating the twin who'd let the new kid nearly cause a pileup, and Maeve was nowhere to be seen.

Cassandra shook her head. "You're like a bad luck charm," she muttered, but it almost sounded like she felt guilty about it.

"Well, you're—"

Before Parker could fill in the blank, Cassandra's horse

squealed, rearing up on its back legs like something out of a movie. Its front hooves pawed the air, and Parker stumbled back as the other girls gasped. Cassandra leaned forward, hugging her horse's neck, her mouth open in surprise as the horse landed back on the ground and immediately leaped right back up in the air like a rodeo horse. All the campers screamed and called for Beth as Cassandra's mount bucked and reared, snorting and twirling. With a particularly savage buck, the horse threw Cassandra into the air. For a moment, she almost seemed to float as she arced right over the horse's head, but then she slammed down, hard.

Everyone leaped off their horses and ran over to where Cassandra lay in the grass.

She wasn't moving, and Beth urged the girls to stand back as she spoke to Cassandra in a gentle voice and felt along her body. For a long moment, Parker's wild imagination took her through every eventuality, most of them ending in Cassandra being paralyzed or dead. She couldn't believe what her last words to her cabinmate would've been if she'd finished that sentence. Tears pricked at her eyes. Even if she hated Cassandra, she didn't deserve . . . that.

"I'm okay," Cassandra said weakly.

Everyone heaved a collective sigh. Beth made sure Cassandra could wiggle her fingers and toes, and that's when Cassandra gasped and sucked in a breath. "My right arm," she said. "It hurts really bad."

Beth frowned as she felt along the dirt-stained arm. "Might

be broken," she said. "But there's no blood. You're going to be okay. Think you can stand up?"

Cassandra nodded and, with help, got back on her feet. Her horse was grazing ten feet away as if nothing had happened at all.

"I've been riding Ginger for years," she said. "She's never done anything like that."

Once Cassandra was up and functional, Beth walked over to the horse, Ginger, approaching the quietly grazing animal with the caution she would show a wild tiger, something that would act unpredictably. The horse just stared at her like she was an idiot and walked over, twitching her tail, long blades of grass poking out of her mouth. Beth held her reins and ran her hands all over the horse's body.

"Maybe there was a wasp or a hornet," she said as she led the now placid horse back over to the group. "I couldn't find a bite, but I've owned Ginger since she was three, and you're right—she's never done anything like that."

"Maybe someone shot a BB gun," one of the twins offered.

Beth frowned. "Not out here. There are fences everywhere. No one would do that."

Maeve appeared at the edge of the forest, and she must've recognized that something was wrong, as she took off running to meet them. Beth filled her in, and Maeve freaked out— because Cassandra was her cousin, after all.

"We've got to get you to the hospital or your mom's gonna kill me," she said.

Cassandra glanced fearfully at Parker. "Uh, it's okay. I'm fine."

"Cass, the only reason anyone ever holds their arm like that is because it's broken. You need to get it checked out. Now, come on." Maeve looked to Beth. "Can your girls get them back to the cabin for me?"

"Of course."

Maeve put her arm around Cassandra and tried to guide her toward the trail, but Cassandra wrenched herself away and turned back to her friends. "Remember what I told you," she said ominously. "Remember the truth."

And then Maeve was hurrying her away.

The other girls cast dubious glances at Parker before turning as one to walk their horses toward the barn. Parker just let Gusty graze until everyone else was grooming. They'd taken up all the halters, and one of the twins had tied up Cassandra's horse, too. Parker remembered—Beth had tied up Gusty inside the barn so she could basically give her a private lesson. She walked her horse through the big open door, grateful for the coolness of the shade—and the way it afforded her some privacy from the distrustful stares of the other girls.

Beth walked in with her own horse, who plodded into a stall and turned around as if accustomed to waiting patiently. "Do you remember what to do?" Beth asked. Parker noted that she looked even more like a mom now: bone-tired and stretched to her limit.

"Curry comb, hard brush, soft brush, legs, hooves," Parker recited.

As Parker ran the plastic curry comb in circles over her sleeping horse's sides, Beth sat down on an overturned bucket, her head in her hands.

"Does this happen a lot?" Parker asked, because it was awkward being alone with an adult's feelings and she knew that her habit of peppering someone with questions would be better than Beth crying.

"Kids getting thrown? No. All of our horses are super gentle and really well cared for." Beth cracked her neck and looked at her hands as if she wished she could've caught Cassandra in midair. "Nothing bad has happened here in a really long time."

This last sentence was curiously ominous. Parker had to know more.

"So . . . what was the last bad thing?"

Beth looked up, her eyes haunted. "I went here when I was a kid, back when it was at the old campus. And . . ."

"And?"

Shaking her head as if to clear it, Beth stood up. "Something bad happened. But then they condemned the old camp and built the new one. We came back the next year, and it was better than ever." She put a hand on Parker's shoulder and did her best to smile. "And aside from college, I've been here every summer since and wouldn't want to be anywhere else. Horses are unpredictable. Just because a fussy mare got stung by a bee doesn't mean you should fear them. You'll get one more trail ride this week. I hope you'll give ol' Gusty another chance."

Parker patted the horse's white fur. His skin twitched as if he was annoyed, so she picked up her hard brush and went back to work. "Sure. I mean, I'll try. But I'm going to start saying whoa a lot earlier next time."

Beth smiled. "Yeah, probably should've warned you about that. He doesn't do that to the little kids—just the older ones, the new ones, when he thinks he can get away with it."

Beth went back outside, and Parker finished grooming Gusty. She wasn't quite ready to pick up his huge hooves by herself, so she headed outside with her hoof pick, hoping one of the twins would help her.

But the other girls from her cabin were whispering, and Parker stopped just inside the door to listen. Maybe it was rude, but at this point, it felt like self-preservation.

"No way, we can't trust her," Addison was saying. "Cassie told us about her, and then she took my necklace, and . . . we just can't."

"But it feels wrong, ignoring her." Parker felt a swell of affection for Kaylee for standing up for her. "Bullying at Camp Care is, like, the opposite of what we do here. It's right there in the name!"

"Well, caring begins with not taking other people's things," Sydney said coldly. "The ball was in her court."

"Maybe she didn't do it." There was a pause, and Parker could imagine everyone looking at poor Kaylee like she was an idiot. "It kind of makes sense, what she said. How would she know about Hanna's lucky scrunchie? And why would she leave everything right on top of her drawer, where we would obviously look first?"

"So who did, then?" Addison asked. "Look around you. You know every single one of us. We all know each other's secrets. We've all slept over at everybody's houses. None of us would take those things." She sounded furious, and Parker could imagine her tanned fingers clutching that necklace as if Parker might show up and try to rip it away from her.

"You know who," Kaylee said quietly. "Gory Tori."

8.

"Come on, Possums! Time to go to lunch!" one of the twins called.

The group outside moved away, muttering to one another, and Parker tossed the hoof pick back in its bucket and followed them down the path. She hoped the next group of kids would go through the same grooming ritual, and someone more experienced would make sure Gusty's feet were good.

As she trailed behind, she noticed Addison repeatedly staring over her shoulder. Parker met her eyes defiantly. No matter what Addison thought, she wasn't a thief, and she wasn't going to skulk around and act like one. With Cassandra out of the picture, her plan was to try to argue her case with them at lunch. Kaylee seemed like she was maybe on Parker's side, or at least not outright against her.

And Gory Tori—who was that, and why would they be sneaking into Possum cabin?

First Beth stopped talking about bad things that had happened in the camp's past right when the story got good, and then the girls got called away before anyone could say more about Gory Tori. It was the worst time for an interruption.

Was Tori some girl from another cabin, or a known camp bully? Maybe someone who used to be part of Possum cabin— but wasn't anymore? Or a counselor everyone was scared of? Was it a boy Tori? A creepy janitor? Parker ached to ask, but admitting to eavesdropping was not going to make the other girls hate her any less.

The twin—Brooke—took them to Friendship Hall. Parker got in line for lunch, always the last one in her cabin, and took her tray to her usual spot beside Jasmine. She had to wait for the right time and place to approach Kaylee, because Parker knew that if she tried to talk to her in front of Addison and Sydney, they would immediately shut it down.

She got her break when most of the group got up to talk to the boys from Badger cabin and Kaylee excused herself to go to the restroom as she did after every meal to check her braces for gross stuff. Once Addison was fully focused on Joshua, her current crush, Parker slipped out of the hall and made a beeline for the bathroom. She found Kaylee leaning over the sink, inspecting her teeth.

"Hey," she said softly.

Kaylee jumped and turned to her. "Hi," she said warily.

"So that was crazy, what just happened to Cassandra, right?"

"Yeah, I guess."

Kaylee went back to poking at her teeth, but Parker was a pro at ignoring social signals.

"Has anything like that ever happened before? I feel like I'm the only person here who doesn't know any of the camp's history." Sure, she'd read every article in the museum off the cafeteria, but Kaylee didn't know that.

Kaylee glanced at the door before giving in. "Nothing like that. These horses are so calm. I take riding lessons back home, and I've never seen such chill, well-behaved horses. I guess Beth said it was a hornet or something." She shrugged. "Horses are unpredictable."

Parker looked in her own mirror, not that she was worried about stuff in her teeth. She needed to get Kaylee talking in the right direction, and not about horses. "I thought I heard that it might be someone named Tori?"

"Oh." Kaylee cleared her throat and looked away just a little too quickly. "I mean, nobody knows for sure, so it's probably just a rumor . . . but people have been whispering about that since we started here."

"See, that's why it's so hard to be the new kid. I don't know all the cool rumors. Is Tori a girl or a boy? Or, like, a local cryptid? Is it a Sasquatch?"

This time, Kaylee didn't just glance at the door. She also squatted to check for feet under the stalls. "We're not supposed to talk about it. If you get caught talking about it, Foggy will call your parents and send you straight home. But everyone says that Gory Tori—"

Kaylee's mouth snapped shut as someone walked in the door and headed for another mirror, a much younger girl from a different cabin. She dug around in her eye for a moment, proudly showed the older girls the crushed bug she'd just pulled out from under her eyelid, and left.

"You were saying?" Parker prompted.

But Kaylee shook her head. "We're not supposed to talk about it. And I'm not willing to risk it." She went back to fishing apple peel out of her braces, and Parker could tell that even for someone who wanted to talk, she was done with that topic.

It sounded like a juicy story, and she wished for ten minutes with fast Wi-Fi to dig around about local lore, but that was the thing about Camp Care: no Wi-Fi, no laptop, no Google. Here, it was all about the people. Of course Parker had researched Camp Care online before coming here, but the website was ancient and bare bones, and all the search results were about great things that happened here, nothing creepy or dangerous at all. And while Parker had Kaylee on her own, she had something else she needed to know.

"Poor Cassandra. I hope her arm is okay," she started.

"She said she'd be back tonight, but I don't know . . ." Kaylee turned toward the door as if worried that Cassandra might waltz in and see her talking to the cabin pariah.

Parker stepped slightly in front of her. "So you've known her forever, right? She just got to my school last year and immediately joined the most popular clique. I've never seen her with glasses before—she must wear contacts at school."

At that, Kaylee cocked her head. "Contacts? No way. She's squeamish about her eyes. She's had glasses since kindergarten. She even had to wear an eye patch for a year."

Parker silently tucked that away for later. "I, uh, actually was worried the whole cabin would be a mean-girl clique, you know? Because that's what Cassandra is like at my school. She . . ." Saying it out loud made her hunch her shoulders as her face grew hot. "She kind of bullied me. Or cyberbullied me? It was this whole thing."

Kaylee stepped forward, looking sincerely shocked. "Cassie? A bully? That's crazy. She got bullied at our old school! It's part of why she moved. They called her Cyclops because of the eye patch, and they just never let it go. Even though she had our troop, and even though Addison always defended her, it just killed her. Cassie would never hurt someone else like that. Although she has been acting kind of different this year . . ."

Parker was trying to imagine a version of Cassandra DiVecchio that was tender and small and crying, but she flat-out couldn't picture it. Cassandra was hard and cold like a diamond, and even if she'd seemed human for a few minutes while they were eating ice cream, Parker had quickly learned that it was all a ruse to keep her occupied while KJ destroyed her life upstairs. Still, Kaylee didn't seem like the sort of person who would lie about that.

Cassandra, on the other hand . . .

"You know I'm not a klepto, right?"

Kaylee looked down; Parker could feel her softening up.

"It . . . doesn't really make sense to me. I don't know when you would've been in the cabin alone, and there's no way you could know about Hanna's scrunchie."

Parker had to hold herself back from getting loud, which she tended to do when excited. It was just so nice to hear someone admit she might not be a thief. "Right? And why would I put everything in my top drawer if I was actually trying to steal stuff?" She glanced at the door, making sure they were alone again. "So you think it might've been Tori?"

Before Kaylee could answer, a shadow fell over her. Addison stood in the bathroom door looking like a vengeful goddess out of a mythology book. The rest of the cabin was arrayed behind her.

"Kaylee, are you sure you want to talk about that right now?" Addison asked.

Kaylee glanced nervously from Addison to Parker. "I mean, she has a right to know the same things we already know. It's got to be hard, being a new person here."

"But remember what Cassie told us," Sydney piped up.

With an inhale, Kaylee drew herself up taller. "I don't know if I agree with that. The evidence suggests that it wasn't Parker. This is Camp Care, and we're supposed to welcome new people. To care about them. So I think we should give Parker a chance."

The other girls shared furtive glances and whispered. Parker put on her brightest smile.

"I'm just a normal kid. I'm not a klepto. I think you're all really cool and I just wish I could hang out with you and have fun. Really."

Addison's mouth twitched. "It was a pretty stupid place to leave our stuff, like whoever put it there wanted it to be found." She turned to the rest of the group. "Let's give her a chance. At least for today. Okay?"

"I don't know . . ." Sydney started.

"It's just one day," Kaylee said. "Besides, if Parker stays with us every moment, and our stuff still disappears, we'll know it's not her."

Most of the girls nodded, although Parker noticed Sydney just shook her head.

Addison turned to her, looking stern. "Parker, do you swear to never be in the cabin alone? And to stop trying to get Kaylee in trouble by talking about literally the only forbidden topic here?"

Parker wanted to salute, but she could tell that was probably too much. "I swear." She held out her pinkie as she had with Jenny, and Addison wrapped her own pinkie around it.

"Okay, then let's get back to the caf. It's almost time for our next activity. We're all really hoping it's canoeing."

"I've always wanted to learn how to canoe," Parker said, beaming, following Addison out of the bathroom with all the other girls. "I read that some Inuit canoes are made of whalebone and have sails made out of seal intestine."

"Well, ours are just fiberglass, but it's still pretty fun," Addison said with a smile. "So you know a lot of random facts, huh?"

"It's kind of my thing."

"You're going to love Saturday—it's trivia night."

"And Friday is Pancake Night!" Kaylee chimed in.

It felt so good, just the simple act of walking from the bathroom to the main hall—because she was in a group. Parker was just another kid in Possum cabin. She promised herself she wouldn't say or do anything stupid. Maybe if she could win the other girls over, the rest of the week wouldn't be so lonely, even if Cassandra came back. Back home, she was known as a know-it-all, a chatterbox, a teacher's pet, a weirdo. But maybe here she could just be the girl in Possum cabin who was great at trivia.

With Maeve at the hospital with Cassandra and Jasmine running her activity, Brooke must've been acting as their interim counselor. She cheerfully chatted with the girls as she led them through the forest, but the mood was definitely less bouncy than usual. It didn't improve when Brooke turned down a twisty trail. The other girls groaned, and someone said, "Really? Now?"

Parker had enjoyed everything they'd done so far— well, she would've enjoyed the lake if not for what had happened there—but the other girls were even more disappointed than they'd been when hiking with Terry.

"It's important to learn this stuff," Brooke reminded them. "Might as well get your money's worth at wilderness camp, right?"

The answer was a resounding, "No!"

An ancient cabin in a small clearing came into view. It wasn't made of modern boards like the other cabins and the main hall but was, rather, constructed of old gray logs with reddish clay gluing them together. There were several mysterious stations set up around what was essentially the cabin's yard. Director Fogarty emerged from the cabin, grinning.

"It's my favorite Possums!" he cried. "Who's ready to learn wilderness skills?"

Parker was utterly gobsmacked when the other girls all cried out, "Me!" as if they hadn't dragged their feet and whined all the way here. They must've really wanted to stay on Foggy's good side—or at least not make him mad.

There were ten stations for the ten—now nine—girls, with a couple of younger counselors floating around to help. Director Fogarty himself joined Parker at her first station, which was just a bunch of rope lying around.

"Knot tying!" he said with more cheerfulness than anyone should feel about some old rope. He took up a piece of rope, nodded for her to do the same, and tried his best to teach her how to make some knots. Much like everything else at camp, she wasn't immediately good at it and therefore did not enjoy it.

"Practice," he said with a wink. "Just master the bow hitch, and you've got everything you need!"

There was this certain thing that a certain kind of adult did, where they acted like they were happier and more excited than

they really were, and it always made Parker deeply uncomfortable in the same way that restaurant waiters singing "Happy
Birthday" did. Foggy hadn't done it when they'd talked in the
commissary and museum, but he was definitely doing it now.
The fact that he was focusing on her in particular only made
his forced exuberance all the creepier. But she also knew that
this particular kind of adult would launch into frowny-faced
concern if she didn't meet their cheerfulness halfway, so she
tried to be a good sport.

At the next station, they dipped candles, which was kind
of fun but took forever. They put up two kinds of tents and
cooked eggs over a fire and looked at moss on trees to deter-
mine directions and built a snare, although they were sternly
reminded not to use any snares on camp property. One whole
station was about never eating mushrooms you found in the
wild, but Parker did enjoy seeing the poisonous mushrooms
Foggy had in sealed ziplock bags.

And then she got to the fire-making station.

She'd read about making fires in plenty of books and
thought she would finally be good at something, but she was
dead wrong. No matter how hard she twisted the stick back
and forth, she couldn't get even the barest wisp of smoke.
When Foggy did it, it worked, but when she did it, it felt like
trying to write with her left hand.

"Don't worry," he said with another creepy wink. "It takes
everybody a couple of years to figure it out. I'm sure you'll get
it next year!"

"I don't think I'll be back next year," she grumbled.

His smile finally broke. "Why not? Everybody always wants to come back."

Parker looked around the clearing, but everyone was out of earshot and dealing with their own challenges. "Well, first of all, I'm here on scholarship. And second of all, someone in my cabin told a lie about me, and the other girls aren't sure how to feel about me. They're warming up, but . . ."

But things might change when Cassandra came back, not that she was telling him that.

Foggy's mouth was hanging open as if this was the most shocking and preposterous thing he'd ever heard.

"Nonsense! This is Camp Care! Everyone gets a fresh start here. We get plenty of scholarship kids with behavior issues—"

Parker angrily twisted the stick harder, faster. "I don't have behavior issues. *I was bullied.* Didn't they tell you that?"

"Well, no." Foggy looked momentarily old and confused, but then he stuck out his chin. "I've known all of these girls forever—some of their parents, too. They're good girls—the best. But it's normal to be shy. Have you tried asking them questions? People love to talk about themselves."

It took everything Parker had not to roll her eyes. "Yeah, I've tried."

Foggy laughed as if that was funny. "Well, I wish I could be Mrs. Piggle-Wiggle and fix it with magic, but part of sleep-away camp is figuring things out yourself, finding your own path. What's your favorite thing that's happened so far?"

Before Cassandra's accident, Parker would've said horseback riding, but now she said, "Well, I did meet this girl at the campfire who seemed really nice, but she's in another cabin."

"Oh? Which one?"

"I forgot to ask. Maybe I could move to her cabin instead?"

Foggy put on that pouty face adults use when telling toddlers they can't have more crackers. "Sorry, honey, but we're totally booked. With a wait list. There isn't a single free bed in camp. But remember: challenges are how life helps us grow. Now, let's put down that stick and go make a compass out of things you can find right here in the woods!"

With that annoying bit of wisdom about challenges, the exclamation points came back in full force, and Parker understood that Foggy, much like her school counselor, could not truly fathom her problem, much less help her find a solution to it. He probably just smiled and smoothed over all the terrible things that happened here and purposely ignored anything negative that didn't directly become his problem.

As Parker moved through the stations, feeling clumsy and ignorant as she approached each new skill under the watchful eye of her least favorite kind of adult, the rest of her cabin was just a little more friendly. Addison complimented her candles, and Charlotte commiserated when her compass wouldn't quite work. When Zoe managed to get a tiny fire going, Parker clapped and hooted along with everyone else. It might've seemed like a simple enough scene, but for Parker, just feeling like she was a part of things was a revelation.

When they were finally done and the xylophone dinged, she thanked Foggy for his help before gladly turning her back on wilderness skills and walking away with her cabin instead of trailing behind them.

Brooke led them back toward the main trail, but no one had the energy to pester her about what they were doing next. Twirling that stick to make a fire had sucked the life right out of them. No one complained when Brooke guided them around the main hall to do tie-dye on the covered back porch.

It was the perfect kind of activity, with everyone crowding around the bins of colorful dye to dip their shirts and pillow-cases. They chattered excitedly about the colors and enthused over the results. Parker happily blended in, being sure not to crowd anyone or stand out too much, although she couldn't stop herself from telling the other girls about how purple dye used to be made from rare seashells and red dye sometimes came from beetles. Each time someone met her eyes and smiled, Parker smiled back. She complimented Zoe on her braids and told Charlotte she loved her mismatched socks. No one shunned her or made fun of her. It was awesome.

When they'd hung up their work to dry on the clotheslines stretching across the yard, the counselor called them back onto the porch to practice Hula-Hooping and teetering on balance boards and juggling hankies and making giant bubbles. Each girl took a turn standing in a tub of soapy liquid in her bare feet while the counselor created a gigantic bubble around her. When it was Parker's turn, she felt just like a picture from a

glossy brochure: happy, smiling, laughing, encased in irides-
cent colors as her friends watched and clapped. Addison offered her some tips on juggling, and when Hanna asked her to
hold one side of the ropes for double Dutch, she gladly took
a longer turn than usual. Parker wished that afternoon could
go on forever, but then the xylophone dinged for quiet time
before dinner.

This time, Parker didn't turn her back to the rest of the
room. Sure, they were reading a different book, but they were
still reading, and no one was shooting her dirty glances. At
dinner, she didn't sit on the other side of a counselor—she sat
with the other Possums and they all brainstormed skits they
could do for Skit Night and even decided to use one of Parker's
ideas about hiking with Terry. When they hit the bathroom
together, she just naturally went along. Most of the stalls were
occupied, and she was going to use the last one, which was
open, but Kaylee put a hand on her arm.

"We don't use that one," she said quietly.

"Why not?"

Kaylee looked slightly embarrassed. "I guess it's kinda
superstition. The light is always out or flickering. There's this
old rumor that if you use the last stall and the light goes out
while you're in there, you're going to die."

Parker stared down at that last stall, the hairs on her arms
rising. As she watched, the flickering fluorescent went dark.
Something dripped down there, the sound echoing back. "Has
anyone ever . . . died at camp?"

"Just one person," Kaylee started. "They say that—"

"Come on, Possums!" Jasmine called from outside. "It's movie night!"

Even if Parker was having a great time being part of her cabin, she was still really excited to see Jenny at the campfire. Maybe the other Possums were now giving her a chance, but Jenny had liked her from the start.

As they left Friendship Hall to head for the campfire circle, Addison whooped and burst into a run. The rest of the cabin followed, all jumping and skipping and screeching with joy. All the other kids in the camp joined in, shouting and wiggling like a thousand happy puppies.

There on the path stood Maeve, and beside her was Cassandra, sporting a hot-pink cast.

9.

Parker was glad Cassandra was okay, but she definitely wasn't overjoyed to see the person who had now ruined her life twice returning as a hero right as she was making headway with the rest of her cabin. As Maeve held out a handful of Sharpies and everyone jockeyed to sign Cassandra's cast, Parker hung back, sitting on the hall's stairs. She couldn't even begin to imagine what it would feel like to have a hundred kids that happy to see her. She couldn't imagine even two.

Addison emerged from the crowd and walked over to Parker. "So are you and Cassie going to make up now?" she asked, twirling the star pendant back and forth.

Parker sighed. "If she'll admit she lied about me, sure."

Addison went from friendly to combative in a heartbeat. "Look, I've known Cassie DiVecchio all my life, and she's not a liar. Like, not one lie in ten years. We want to give you a chance, but—"

Parker jumped up, her hands in fists. "But in order for you to give me that chance, I have to lie and say I'm a klepto? I'm just supposed to pretend I'm a bad person if I want to be friends with you guys? So you can go on believing that Cassandra is a nice girl instead of a bully? Those are the conditions of your friendship? That I tell an actual lie? About myself?"

Now Addison stepped closer, threatening. "Cassie is not a bully. She's the kind of person who *gets* bullied! I told everyone we should get to know you, but if you think she's a bully, then you're not worth getting to know. Don't talk to me again. Don't talk to any of us." She shook her head in disgust and headed back to where the other girls of Possum cabin were watching, eyes wide, whispers rampant behind their hands.

Parker slumped back down on the stairs. Possum cabin turned their backs on her, with only Kaylee looking as if she felt bad about it. If the only options were to pretend that she was a thief and maybe be accepted or to stand up for who she was and be rejected as usual, then there was no question. Parker wanted friends, but not at the expense of her integrity.

Soon the counselors urged people to take their Sharpies and their energy down to the campfire circle. It was movie night, whatever that meant, and the scent of fresh popcorn was floating out of the kitchens. With all the hubbub over Cassandra, the counselors had given up on trying to separate out their cabins, so Parker trudged along behind the huge clot of kids and small groupings of laughing teens.

When they got to the campfire circle, there was no fire,

nor were the usual rolling coolers of s'more ingredients present. Instead, a giant white screen was tied tightly between the trees behind the blackened firepit. The kids separated into their usual cabins, but this time they sat on blankets spread out in front of their benches. The counselors carried around big cardboard boxes and passed out paper bags of hot popcorn. It would've been really, really cool if Parker hadn't felt like the dog poop on the bottom of the camp's sneaker.

Everyone was still fawning over Cassandra. There were so many signatures that her cast was starting to look more black than pink. The movie flickered to life on the screen—*Lilo and Stitch*—and Parker felt a little lift. She loved this movie. She . . . identified with Lilo a lot.

As soon as everyone was focused on the movie, Parker stood up and wandered back toward the tree line with her popcorn. Just as she'd hoped, Jenny was waiting there, sitting on the grass with her arms around her knees. They were farther from the screen, but with everyone else spread out below them, Parker could see the movie clearly instead of leaning from side to side to see over the heads of the taller kids in front.

"I didn't know if you would come," Jenny said, as twitchy as a stray cat.

"Of course! I've been looking forward to hanging out. It was the worst day ever."

Jenny's dark eyes gleamed with sympathy. "Yeah?"

With that prompt, with that barest bit of understanding, it was like Parker's floodgates opened. "We were riding horses, and my horse was acting up, and then Cassandra's horse bucked and threw her. And, I mean, I hate her, but it was kind of terrifying? For, like, a minute, we thought she was dead. She went to the hospital, and the rest of my cabin was actually nice to me. With Cassandra gone, they were willing to let me be a part of things, and it was really fun. But then Addison asked me if I was going to get along with Cassandra, and I told her I would if Cassandra would admit she lied about me. She said that Cassandra doesn't lie, and that she's not a bully, and now she told everyone in my cabin not to talk to me. I thought Addison was nice when I got here, but it turns out she's a bully, too."

Jenny trembled with rage, her eyebrows drawn down and her mouth screwed up. "That's not fair. First Cassandra bullied you, and now Addison. That shouldn't happen here. It shouldn't be allowed."

"I know! But that's the thing about bullying, isn't it? Adults always say they'll help, but then they don't. It's like they think a bully is this tall kid who punches you in front of everyone in the hallway for your lunch money, when really it's a pretty girl with a smile saying things that could almost sound nice if she wasn't sneering." She pulled her knees up, too, and played with the friendship bracelet Jenny had given her. She could see the one she'd given Jenny, in a place of pride on top of all Jenny's other, much fancier bracelets.

"But sometimes bullies get what they deserve," Jenny said. Parker couldn't see her too well in the dark, sitting next to her, but she could tell Jenny was smiling.

"Not usually," Parker replied with a small shrug. "I mean, even if I hate Cassandra, I wouldn't wish what happened on her. I'm not a bad person. I just want her to leave me alone." She rubbed at a splotch of dye on her sneaker toe. "I used to want her to like me, but it turns out she's just like everybody else."

"They try to be your friend first," Jenny agreed. "They make you believe. Then when they tell you to do something, you just do it. Because it feels good when they finally seem to see you. And that's when they can hurt you the most."

"Right?" Parker was nodding along—Jenny had said it perfectly. "That's what happened with Cassandra originally. I thought she was being nice to me, but she was only doing it to distract me so her friends could steal my stuff. And then I thought Addison was being nice to me, but just now, she was like a totally different person." She fidgeted with her bracelet. "At least you and I get to hang out. I wish we were in the same cabin."

"Me too. That would've been rad."

For a while, they just watched the movie. Parker offered Jenny some of her popcorn, but Jenny shook her head. It was really nice, actually, sitting outside in a forest on a nice, breezy night, watching one of her favorite movies, sitting side by side with a friend. At one point, Parker's skin crawled, and when she looked away from the screen, Cassandra and Addison were both turned around, glaring at her. Smirking back at them, she waved like the queen.

"That's them," she said to Jenny. "Cassandra and Addison."

"Oh, I know," Jenny said. "If you stay here long enough, you know everybody."

Cassandra and Addison rolled their eyes and shook their heads and turned back around.

"They look like angry horses," Jenny said.

Parker laughed so hard she almost choked on popcorn, and the nearest campers turned around to shush her.

When the end credits started, Jenny said, "I'll see you later, right? Tomorrow night?"

"Hopefully earlier," Parker said with a sigh. "I can't believe I'm this lonely surrounded by this many people."

"I totally know that feeling. Oh! And I meant to give you this." Jenny took off another friendship bracelet, this one in tones of blue.

Parker held out her wrist, and Jenny tied it on beside the pink one.

"Oh my gosh, it's so pretty! I wish I had another one to give you, but we haven't been back to the crafts cabin."

Jenny held out her pinkie, grinning. "That's okay. You'll have time."

Parker's heart felt warm as she hooked her pinkie around Jenny's. Having a friend, a true friend, really did feel as wonderful as she'd always hoped.

"Best friends?" Jenny asked.

"Best friends!" Parker happily responded.

Parker rejoined her cabin as Jenny waited under the trees. Even if Possum cabin was pretending she didn't exist, Parker

kind of felt like she was wearing armor as she fell in line behind Jasmine and followed the crowd back to the cabins. Sure,
these girls could continue to shun her, but she now knew there
was at least one person who genuinely saw her and cared that
she was here, and that was enough.

All the way back to the cabin, kids were still buzzing
around Cassandra, asking her about the accident and signing
her cast and hoping out loud that they wouldn't be assigned
to ride Ginger.

"They might shut down horseback riding," one girl said,
tossing a long red braid over her shoulder.

"No way," said another. "There've been horses here since
it opened."

"Maybe they'll rebuild the barn somewhere else," a gangly
boy with glasses said. "Like they did last time."

That caught Parker's attention. She had to assume he
was talking about whatever had happened in 1988, and she was
dying to ask if the mysterious tragedy had occurred at the
barn. That might explain why Beth had looked so worried and
scared—they might fire her or sell her horses and close down
the barn permanently. She stayed close to keep listening, but
Sydney elbowed the gangly boy and said, "Shhh. Foggy might
hear you."

"Or worse," teased the girl with the braid. "*Gory Tori
might hear you*. A girl in my cabin used the last bathroom stall
on a dare, and the light went out while she was in there, and
she said she heard footsteps in the forest the other night—"

"Maddie!" a counselor barked.

The girl with the braid looked absolutely terrified as she went silent, then muttered, "Sorry."

At that, the other girl and boy grimaced and faded back into the crowd. Parker thought about trying to find one of them later and ask some pertinent questions, but then she remembered that her cabinmates had probably told everybody here about the lying klepto they were stuck with. That would explain why no one else ever smiled at her and why girls generally steered around her in the bathroom. That was another thing about bullying: when it turned into a whisper network, when everybody else was against you, it was like fighting smoke. Her golden afternoon of normalcy was definitely over.

Getting ready for bed wasn't too horrible, as everyone was still cooing over Cassandra and offering to brush her hair or put toothpaste on her toothbrush like she was a little baby. No one paid any attention to Parker as she brushed her teeth and tromped back to Possum cabin in her pajamas. She was in bed before everyone else, trying to escape into her book while the lights were still on. It was almost impossible to focus. Each time someone in her novel mentioned their horse, all Parker could think about was Cassandra flying out of the saddle like a crash test dummy and lying so still on the ground afterward.

Parker slept pretty well at camp, even if the bed wasn't as comfortable as her big, soft, cozy one at home. The nights were cool, and soft breezes wafted through the screened windows all around the room. It probably helped that by the end of every day, she was physically and mentally exhausted. The first two nights, it was as if her head hit the pillow and then she woke up to the honking trumpet.

But tonight, for some reason, she startled awake. Her eyes popped open, and she tried to figure out what had roused her. She was on her side, sheet pulled up over her shoulder, just the right temperature. There were no sounds but the leaves rustling outside and eleven people softly breathing. Nothing moved—

Except, yes, something moved.

The screen door should've been latched, but it wasn't. It was open just a few inches, swaying gently. It was dark by the door, the moon hidden behind the clouds, and it looked as if something had spilled on the floorboards—a puddle of water, maybe. As Parker watched, unmoving, trying not to breathe, she heard a faint dripping noise.

Someone was standing there in the dark, just standing there in their Camp Care uniform. And something wet was dripping down from their hands.

Parker's sleep-addled brain tried to puzzle it out. Maybe one of the girls had gone to the bathroom, or run out in a brief rain-storm? Or maybe they'd snuck out to play in the lake? Maybe this was some sick joke, like the girls in her cabin were trying to scare her into leaving. Or maybe one of them was framing her as Cassandra had, trying to get her into big enough trouble that she'd get sent immediately home.

"Hello?" she called softly. "I can see you."

The figure began to turn, lifting one dripping hand, and—

"Pillow fight!" someone shouted.

The door banged open and bounced off the wall. In charged ten girls in their pajamas holding pillows and shrieking. Someone hit the lights, and the rest of Possum cabin erupted out of their beds, grabbed their own pillows, and began swinging. Parker could only watch, stunned, as feathers filled the air and nineteen girls screeched like banshees.

She leaned down to look into Jasmine's bunk. Jasmine was awake, smiling, arms crossed, watching the pillow fight like a tired mama cat.

"Are they allowed to do this?" Parker asked.

Jasmine shrugged. "Happens every week, every year. As long as it's not boy-girl, nobody tells Foggy, and nobody gets in trouble. You should join in. It's fun."

But Parker knew better than to try. Getting rejected from a group pillow fight would just be embarrassing. As it was, no one was paying her any attention at all. The other campers didn't approach her bunk, and she didn't climb down to see if they'd let her participate. She just watched from the outside, as she always did. Other than getting hit in the face with a firm pillow, which sent Kaylee sprawling to the ground, it looked like a lot of fun.

After a few minutes of chaos, all the invading girls fist-bumped the Possum campers and left. The last one turned out the light, and Addison latched the screen door shut behind them.

"Back in bed, Possums!" Maeve called from her bunk. "Trumpet's gonna toot tomorrow whether you're ready or not!"

It took a long time for everyone to settle down again—they were all amped up by the high-adrenaline raid. But Parker was more concerned with what had originally caused her to pop awake. When the lights were on, she hadn't seen anything over by the screen door—no mysterious person, no wet spot where she'd definitely seen a dark, spreading puddle.

She must've been dreaming, or having sleep paralysis, or something, because she was certain she'd seen someone there. She stared at the door for so long without blinking that her eyes watered down her cheek onto her pillow. She just couldn't bring herself to turn away, to stop watching that door. At some point, she fell asleep, but she didn't sleep well. She tossed and turned and kicked off her covers. There were crunches outside, odd rustles, creaking doors, dripping sounds even though it wasn't raining. The forest wasn't soothing and calm; it was full of secrets and shadows, waiting to consume her. When the trumpet finally bleated, it was almost a relief to stop trying to stay under.

It was a bright day, and the cabin was aglow with morning sun. White and brown feathers dusted the floor, but over by the door, there was nothing to indicate there had ever been a puddle of water.

"Did you leave the door unlatched last night?" she asked Jasmine while the other girls descended on the bathroom to get ready.

Jasmine frowned. "No. They usually knock, and someone lets them in. You can't just pop it open from outside."

"But they just ran in."

Jasmine walked over to the door and fiddled with the latch. "Huh. It seems totally normal. Although—ew. What?"

She pulled back her hand from the doorknob, and there was a smear of red on it.

Whatever it was . . . it looked like blood.

10.

Parker was pretty freaked out by the blood on Jasmine's hand—because what else would it be? How many opaque red liquids were there in the world, much less at a summer camp in the middle of nowhere? But Jasmine said it was probably paint or dye from tie-dyeing or lipstick or nail polish, or maybe one of the campers had snagged her hand on a nail or something during the skirmish. She wiped it off on her shorts as if it was nothing.

But Parker knew she'd seen something no one else had seen, that hunched shape lurking in the shadows, liquid dripping to puddle on the floor.

"What if it's . . . Gory Tori?" Parker whispered.

Jasmine winced. "Where'd you hear about that? Never mind. I don't want to know. Definitely don't talk about that again. There are rules, and then there are Rules with a capital *R*, and that one will get you kicked out. It's just a stupid story some kids made up. It's not real."

"How do you know?"

Jasmine sighed and rolled her eyes. "I've been going here since I was six, every year, and then two full summers as a counselor, and I've never heard any facts, seen any evidence, or even been able to patch together a story that made any sense. It's just two words that kids whisper when they want to seem cool and scare the first graders, because every sleepaway camp ever has to have its own dumb rumor."

"But I saw something last night . . ." Parker trailed off, uncertain how much she could say before Jasmine would decide she was crazy, or just trying to get attention. Or, if she still believed whatever rumors Cassandra was spreading, that Parker was a liar.

"Look, even if there was a ghost or a serial killer or whatever this year's kids say it is, it would have to be super old. This isn't even the original camp. It's all the way on the other side of the lake, and nothing bad has ever happened on this side of the fence. So unless you saw a 1950s ghost in a poodle skirt on a glowing blue bicycle, I don't know how it got over here." When Parker's head drooped, Jasmine put a hand on her shoulder. "Hey. I know you're having a rough time. That doesn't happen much here, and Foggy wants us to pretend it never does. It's got to be hard being the new kid in a cabin of BFFs. But trust me: talking about Gory Tori is not going to win you friends."

That wasn't what Parker was doing at all, but she knew how conversations like this one went. If she kept prying and pushing, Jasmine would get more and more closed off, and then she wouldn't have a single person in her cabin who didn't straight-up hate her.

Still, she wanted to know more about Gory Tori. Jasmine had mentioned ghosts and serial killers, and Parker adamantly didn't believe in ghosts. She'd done some deep research for a big science project, and she simply wasn't convinced. And if Tori was a serial killer, there would have to be dead bodies, which meant parents wouldn't keep sending their precious darlings to camp. None of it added up, but Kaylee was definitely scared of something—and Foggy definitely didn't want people to talk about it, whatever it was.

As soon as the other campers returned, Parker had her stuff ready and scuttled over to the bathroom to shower and get dressed on her own. Even if all the hot water was long gone, a cold shower was more pleasant than hearing them whisper about her.

There were waffles and bacon for breakfast, and as she chewed, Parker scanned the cafeteria to identify the cabin that had raided them last night. They were across the hall, just a table of girls like any other, eating and chatting and laughing. From time to time, some of the girls would get up to fetch something off the buffet and swerve around to interact with the boys. Parker wasn't even going to try. If Cassandra and Addison had told everyone in camp to ignore her, she'd rather be ignored than have the boys actively against her or trying to mess with her. Her idle dreams of flirting with or even kissing a boy this summer had long since fled. She would settle for not being embarrassed by one or in front of one.

Soon the xylophone *bing*ed, and Possum cabin's first activity was fishing, which was fun but a little boring. They were each given an old fishing rod and the bait of their choice, and everyone else seemed to know exactly what to do with these materials, whereas Parker just stood on the dock in her stinky life jacket, holding her fishing rod and staring at bread, corn, hot dogs, worms, and minnows set out like the world's grossest buffet.

"Ever fished before?" the counselor asked. Her name was Susan, and she was younger than most of the other counselors and looked like Velma from *Scooby-Doo*.

"Just once, on a boat in St. Augustine."

Susan looked Parker up and down as if she was fitting her for a dress instead of teaching her how to fish. "Better go with bluegills, then." She grabbed a piece of bread and led Parker up the dock toward the shore.

Most of the other girls were as far away from the land as they could get, sitting on the dock but careful to keep their feet out of the water so they wouldn't disturb the fish. Even with her cast, Cassie could fish like that, with the girls on either side of her promising that if she got something on the hook, they'd help her pull it up. Addison stood at the farthest end of the dock, throwing her bobber out as far as she could before reeling it back in. Shut must've sensed Parker watching her, as she glanced over and tossed her ponytail in annoyance.

Susan stopped and showed Parker how to drop her line in the green water under the dock, where dark shadows flickered back and forth: the bluegills. It was kind of fun, actually, letting her hook sink under the surface and watching the fish pluck at the tight ball of bread Parker had carefully speared on the hook. She got a bite relatively quickly, but she didn't jerk back fast enough, so the bluegill got away. With Susan's help, she soon had her first fish on the line.

"First catch of the day!" Susan crowed.

The other girls turned around excitedly until they saw who it was, then they turned back to watch their own bobbers. Addison had clearly spread the word that Parker was a pariah again.

As she showed Parker how to get the fish off her hook, Susan muttered, "So you're the lowest one in the pecking order, huh? Always happens to the new kid. I started here in fourth grade and felt like an alien. But by fifth grade, I was hooked. Just stick with it, okay? They'll come around, I promise."

Parker wasn't so sure, but she wasn't going to tell Susan that. It was so easy to think it might happen, to fantasize about coming back next year and not being a stranger. But she was pretty sure Susan's cabin hadn't had its own version of Cassandra DiVecchio. If it had, Susan definitely wouldn't be here, tossing bluegills back in the lake, when she could be literally anywhere else in the world.

Hanna, Zoe, and Emma each caught a slimy catfish, Charlotte caught a big, nasty carp covered in snot, and Addison had an exciting tug-of-war battle with a bass that broke the line right before she could pull it out of the water. Parker caught two more bluegills, but no one found that exciting. They'd probably been catching bluegills for years, and the catfish and carp were certainly bigger and put up more of a fight. It was peaceful, but Parker still felt a little nervous, being so close to the lake. It was like a constant, worrisome buzz under her skin. Even here, by the shore, it was so deep she couldn't see the sandy bottom. The water was so dark and silty and thick that it reminded her of cocoa, and she couldn't forget the cold, clammy hand that had clutched her ankle and dragged her down without mercy. Even with the sun out, it was creepy and thick with secrets.

By the time the xylophone *bing*ed for the next activity, Parker had that sunny, salty satisfaction she always got near the water, and even if her hands stunk of fish and her shirt smelled like the ancient life jacket that no one else had to wear, it was nice to know that here, finally, was one thing she didn't suck at.

They all fist-bumped Susan and ran ahead to where Maeve beckoned to them from farther up the path. The girls who'd managed to catch fish bragged about it, and the girls who hadn't grumbled about losing their bait and getting caught on logs and other people being too noisy on the dock. Parker didn't need to tell Maeve about her fish, though—not only because she suspected that no one was impressed with bluegills but also because she just didn't think either of her counselors really cared about her the way they cared about the other girls. Even if they cheerfully answered her questions and weren't exactly ignoring her, it was obvious she was in distress and neither of them had made any attempt to fix the problem.

Jasmine had even brought it up earlier—and done nothing about it. And Maeve had been downright cold ever since Parker had accused her cousin of lying. Maybe they'd never been bullied, or maybe they were turning into adults and were realizing that it was simpler just to look the other way and let these things sort themselves out. Maybe they were happy to go along with the popular viewpoint, because it was more comfortable than facing the problem head-on. Maybe it was easier for Maeve to accuse the new kid of being the liar than to consider that someone she loved might secretly go against all the ideals the camp and its employees were supposed to uphold. From their point of view, this annoying little problem would be over in a week anyway. But to Parker, that week felt like a year.

Maeve led them into the forest, and all the other girls cheered when they realized that their next activity was archery. Parker soon understood that this was 50 percent the fun of shooting arrows and 50 percent the hotness of the archery teacher, Grey. Even Maeve lingered longer than usual after dropping them off.

Okay, yes, fine, he was really cute, but he was also practically an adult. Still, watching Addison and Sydney flutter their eyelashes was nauseating, and when Cassandra played up her injury and stuck out her bottom lip for extra attention, Parker literally gagged.

She'd never shot a bow and arrows before, but she'd read tons of books about people who did and liked to think that she would be a prodigy.

As it turned out, she was not.

It was super awkward. As with horseback riding, she had to do several things perfectly all at once, which was really difficult. It took a lot of strength to pull back the bowstring while holding the bow just right and taking aim. Of course the camp had been dealing with new archers for decades, so instead of having little targets pinned to trees, there was a wide plywood wall with big targets set at intervals. Parker was certain that without that long, tall wall, all her arrows would've disappeared into the forest beyond—at least the ones that went far enough.

The other girls were more competent, but even with their experience, most of them didn't hit their target reliably. Addison was the only one who was really, really good, and as much as Parker was starting to hate her, even she had to admit that the tall, tan, blond girl looked like Artemis every time she pulled the string back to her cheek, her face deadly serious.

Under Grey's instruction, the girls divided up into two groups. Each group lined up before the wall, shot their ten arrows apiece, put their bows on the ground, and went to retrieve their color-coded arrows while the other five girls sat on a designated bench. This way, there was absolutely no way anyone could get hurt. Parker had to wonder what archery had been like in the seventies, before people really started taking their kids' safety seriously. In the lawn dart days, did they just hand a bunch of kids their bows and arrows and send them off into the forest to run wild? Even though these were practice arrows with blunted tips instead of sharpened points, they were still hard. When she pulled her first one out of the plywood, she rubbed her thumb over the metal tip and winced.

It didn't take long for Parker to get into the rhythm, and as she waited her turn, she watched the other five girls shoot, trying to glean tips on how to hit her target with better accuracy. She could see that Hanna always looked down at the last minute and that Charlotte pulled her string too far back instead of gently releasing it. But Addison—well, it was like watching a professional. Addison was one of those people who was just better at stuff than everybody else—at least physical stuff. Who knew what she was like at school? Then again, Parker guessed she was a straight-A kid and probably on student council and the founder and president of some club that involved leadership.

Addison shot her last arrow, hitting the bull's-eye, and Grey blew his whistle and called, "Bows down!" The five archers put down their bows, and the other four girls perked up on the bench, eager for their turns. Everyone watched enviously as Addison pulled all ten of her arrows out of her target—not a single arrow had gone wide.

"It's so not fair," Sydney muttered.

"Of course it's fair," Kaylee shot back. "She takes lessons at home. There's no rule against that."

Parker was watching Addison, wondering what it would be like to be that tall and sure of yourself, that well-liked by the people around you. Getting good grades was a private thing, unless you bragged about it, which, yes, Parker probably did too much. But being good at archery or fishing was a public thing, like singing or dancing, and she wanted to know what it would be like to have people watch her do something and be jealous.

And because she was watching Addison so closely, Parker saw the exact moment it happened.

Addison had her back to the group as she pulled her last arrow out of the plywood, and then, suddenly, with no warning whatsoever or even the telltale twang of the string, an arrow thudded into the back of her arm, halfway between her shoulder and her elbow.

For a split second, it wiggled like an antenna.

And then Addison screamed and dropped all her arrows with a clatter, reaching back for the arrow in her arm, scrabbling at it, twisting and turning, not comprehending what had happened. All the other girls started screaming, too, but nobody knew what to do. Charlotte and Hanna tried to help her, fluttering around her and flapping their hands and crying and screaming for Grey, while all the girls who were on the bench stayed there, whispering and giving one another suspicious glances. Most of the suspicious glances focused on Parker, but she had not moved an inch from where she sat.

Then Grey was there, talking softly to Addison, not daring to touch the arrow. He had a walkie-talkie in one of his cargo shorts pockets, and Parker realized that—of course he did. They had to. All these teen counselors, spread out in the huge forest in charge of kids who got injured, had to have a way to communicate other than running and shouting.

Grey had Addison sit on the ground while he barked into the walkie, and she collapsed in the dirt, slumped forward, crying, not daring to look back at the arrow sprouting from her arm. Blood dripped off her elbow, a single rivulet trailing down to her wrist and staining her Camp Care shirt.

"Why doesn't he pull the arrow out?" Kaylee whispered to Sydney.

But Sydney could only shake her head, wide-eyed, so Parker said, "Because you're not supposed to pull stuff out— like, the arrow or knife or whatever. It could be in an artery, and if they pulled it out, she could die. If you ever get stabbed, you should definitely leave the knife in and let the people at the hospital take it out."

Someone gasped. "But she's not going to die?" Kaylee croaked out.

Sydney leaned in front of Parker, blocking her from answering. "Of course not. That's her arm, not her heart or her liver or whatever."

Grey stayed with Addison, ignoring everyone else, until Foggy showed up with the camp nurse on an ATV. Parker hadn't seen the nurse in action before, but she did recognize the twenty-something guy in the blue scrubs from s'mores night.

As the nurse helped Addison onto the ATV, Foggy pulled Grey aside, behind the tiny archery cabin where all the bows and arrows were stored.

"How'd this happen?" Foggy asked. It was clear he was trying to keep his voice down, but they were in a big, empty forest, so of course the girls all heard every word.

"I don't know, sir. Everyone was following the rules exactly. All the bows were on the ground, all the other campers were on the bench, and I was behind the line."

"Have you searched the woods?"

"No, sir. I've been with Addison the whole time. There were no other counselors present."

All the girls exchanged glances during the long pause.

"Figure out what happened," Foggy finally said. "We can't have another big accident. This could've been a lot worse."

"Yes, sir."

"We're ready, Director," the nurse called, and Foggy hurried to the ATV and drove Addison away. All the girls of Possum cabin waved to Addison as the ATV tore down the trail, but she couldn't see them because she was facing forward. Parker couldn't help focusing on the arrow, still obscenely poking out of the girl's arm.

Grey walked over to the bench, looking shaken. "Okay, I think that's enough for today. I'll finish cleaning up the equipment. Did anybody see anything unusual?"

They all shook their heads.

"Was anybody holding a bow?"

A few girls glanced at Parker, as if they'd love to be able to blame it on her, but they'd all seen her sitting on the bench, far from the bows and arrows. And even if she'd been holding one at the time, they'd seen that she had a hard enough time hitting the plywood at all, much less the three-inch-wide strip of a girl's arm.

"I want everybody to go sit on the logs in front of the cabin until Maeve gets back," Grey said. "Just hang out and play Miss Susie or slaps or something."

Parker followed her cabinmates over to the logs, but there wasn't any room for her. The other girls paired off to play games, and Sydney pulled a string out of her pocket to play cat's cradle, but Parker just sat on the ground and stared off into the forest.

She was the only one who saw Grey searching the underbrush in the forest behind the bench.

She was the only one who saw him squat and poke around the ground with a stick.

She was the only one who saw him stand up, holding a bow and quiver where no bow and quiver had any right to be.

11.

Grey didn't say anything to the Possum girls about what he'd found. He slipped into the cabin with the bow and quiver, and Parker heard him speaking hurriedly on the walkie, although she couldn't make out any actual words. Soon Maeve arrived, and the girls all tumbled over one another to tell her what had happened and how scary it had been. Maeve hugged Cassandra and told her she was so glad she'd been on the sidelines with her cast instead of out there when it had happened. After speaking briefly with Grey in the archery cabin, Maeve quick-marched the girls back to the main trails, ending up at the art cabin.

"We've got half an hour until lunch, so just chill," Maeve told them nervously. "I've got to go . . . do some stuff."

When Parker had first met her, she'd imagined that every single sentence Maeve said had to end in an exclamation point. But now that two scary, dangerous things had happened, those exclamation points were gone. Now she just seemed spooked.

The art cabin was empty, so the girls found their clipboards and started working on their friendship bracelets. They were quieter than usual, and Parker found it kind of soothing until she realized that it was because they were scared, too.

"This is messed up," Sydney finally said angrily.

"I kinda wanna go home," whispered Rosemary, who barely ever spoke.

"Nothing bad ever happens here," Kaylee said softly. "It never has before."

"I mean, accidents happen." Charlotte always sounded like a teacher, Parker had noticed. "Maybe we were just due."

"But only us—just our cabin? That's illogical." Hanna sighed. "Statistically speaking, it just doesn't make sense."

"Or it's bad luck." Sydney said it so sharply that Parker looked up from the green-and-blue bracelet she was making for Jenny. When Parker met her eyes, Sydney raised her eyebrows. "Almost like we really do have a bad-luck charm this year."

Parker's jaw dropped. "Bad-luck charm? Really? *I* was the first person something bad happened to! Something grabbed me during my swim test, and I almost drowned!"

Sydney gave her biggest eye roll yet. If eye-rolling had been an activity at camp, Sydney would've held the gold medal. "Nothing grabbed you. You said you could swim and you couldn't, and when you failed out, you had to blame it on something. Just like you tried to blame Cassie when you stole our stuff. I bet you shot Addison because she put you in your place."

Everyone looked at Parker, considering this possibility. No one stood up for her. Even Kaylee's mouth was set.

"You know that makes no sense, right?" Parker stood. "First of all, I'm a good swimmer. I swam out to the end of the dock just fine, and then something grabbed me, and the fact that no one believes me is nuts. Second, I clearly can't shoot a bow and arrow! You saw it! I suck at it! Just like I suck at everything else! Third, I was sitting right next to you on the bench! And last, even if I was good at archery, why would I want to hurt someone? If I wanted to hurt someone in our cabin, I would just smother them in their sleep."

"Oh my god, she's *in our cabin while we're asleep*," Rosemary whispered, and Parker instantly realized that even if what she'd said was a good argument, now they were all going to freak out about sleeping in the same room with her.

"Look, I get that you all hate me, but I didn't do any of the things Cassandra said I did. I don't know how to prove it to you. But I saw Grey find a bow and quiver in the forest while you guys were on the logs."

Cassandra hadn't said anything yet, but she seemed to take that part seriously. "And Brooke said maybe it was a BB that made Ginger freak out," she said slowly, ignoring the part about her. "Maybe somebody really is out to hurt us."

"Why?" said Kaylee, throwing her hands in the air. "We've

been coming here forever, and we're just normal campers. We don't have any enemies. This is Camp Care!"

Sydney zeroed in on Parker again. "It has to be the new girl. She's the only thing that's changed."

"Me? Why would anybody want to hurt me?"

"Because people who lie and steal make enemies." Sydney tossed her hair. "We don't like you, and we want you gone. Other people probably feel the same way."

"I'm just a normal twelve-year-old girl!" Parker roared. "The only thing weird about me is that everyone here decided they hated me before they even met me!"

Picking up her clipboard, she stormed out of the cabin and sat on the grass, far enough away that she didn't have to hear what the other girls were saying about her. Her shorts were instantly damp, but she didn't care. She couldn't listen to their gossip anymore. It was cruel and ridiculous and wrong, and the worst part was, they all knew it. And yet no one stood up to Sydney at all. It was just easier to blame Parker than to consider darker possibilities.

Maybe it really was like a sleepaway camp horror movie— maybe some twisted guy in a mask was trying to pick them off one by one from the safety of the forest. Or maybe it was Gory Tori. A ghost could spook a horse, probably, and . . . well, okay, so a ghost probably couldn't shoot a bow and arrow, and Parker still wasn't willing to believe in ghosts. But maybe . . . a demon could possess someone and make them do it? Or maybe Gory

Tori was a dangerous troublemaker, some past camper or angry mountain man who wanted revenge?

There was no good answer for what was happening, but Parker was certain it had nothing to do with her personally. It was her first time here, and she'd never done anything to inspire a desire for revenge in anyone else. Didn't people have to feel deeply about a person to be driven mad enough to cause violence? Yeah, so nobody had ever felt that way about Parker. She was generally the one who got bullied or wronged. As she fumed, she furiously worked on the friendship bracelet and focused on not pulling the embroidery floss too tight. She was getting faster, and when the xylophone rang over the speakers, she took her clipboard with her and ran for Friendship Hall so she could get her food before the rest of her cabin showed up.

This time, she didn't sit next to Jasmine and try to disappear. After looking around for Jenny and not finding her, she ditched her tray and took her food outside, found a nice bench around the side of the hall, and sat down to enjoy her meal alone and work on her bracelet. No one stopped her, but then again, no one really stopped anyone from doing anything. There were rules, but people followed them because they wanted to come back.

Parker now had no interest in coming back.

In fact, the main reason she didn't march into Foggy's office and ask him to call her parents was that it would be embarrassing. Her parents would think she was a big baby, and Cassandra would go home and tell KJ and Olivia that she was a big

baby, and she would feel like a big baby who'd failed her first
real test of adulthood. If little first graders could stay here for a
week, then Parker Nelson could stay here for a week.

And not only that, but she liked Jenny and wanted to hang
out with her more. She needed to get Jenny's number or email
so that they could stay in touch once they went back home.
Maybe Jenny lived close enough to visit. If Parker left now,
she would lose the one good thing about camp and her first
real friend. As she threw her trash away, she again stood in the
doorway and scanned the main hall for Jenny, but as usual,
there was no sign of her. Maybe her cabin ate at a different
time, or maybe she had a medical issue or something.

"Hey."

Parker spun around to find a boy standing there. He wasn't
one of the super-cute guys her whole cabin fawned over at
lunch and flirted with at the campfire, but he had kind eyes
and floppy hair and was smiling at her.

"Hey," she answered, tentatively smiling back and thinking very hard about what might or might not be stuck in her
teeth.

"I'm Mason."

"I'm Parker."

"Oh." His eyes went wide, and he took a step back. "Uh,
never mind." Mason didn't quite run away, but he definitely
walked away faster than he'd approached.

Clearly, Addison and Cassandra had been telling everyone
in camp exactly who to avoid. Parker sat down around the side

of the building and slumped over, forehead on her clipboard. She'd been waiting years for a cute boy she hadn't known since kindergarten to talk to her, and after only three words out of her mouth, the first boy who did disappeared. She spent the rest of lunch working on her bracelet and trying not to cry.

When the xylophone *bing*ed and everyone gathered outside, Maeve asked them, "Are you guys okay to keep doing activities? We can just hang in the cabin if you want."

"No way," said Sydney, who seemed to have stepped in as the leader since Addison was out. "That's boring. And our bad luck would just follow us there." She glanced defiantly at Parker, who couldn't believe how much Sydney's inner mean girl was showing. This camp was supposed to bring out the best in everyone, and Kaylee had said that the other girls were all best friends. But first Addison and now Sydney seemed to be showing their true colors, now that everything wasn't all rainbows.

When Maeve turned down a new path—how had they memorized all these trails?—the girls groaned in unison. Except, oddly, for Sydney, who bounced on her toes a bit.

"Do we have to?" Kaylee whined.

"If we're sticking to our schedule, everybody except Cassie does," Maeve reminded her. "You've got to be ready for Flag Wars on Friday."

Parker wanted to know why a camp focused on caring would have an activity centered on war, but she wasn't about to ask.

Instead of leading them to a clearing with a cabin or equipment stations laid out, this path took them to a patch of forest
with its trees intact but its undergrowth mostly cleared, shorn
down to the ground. Twisted roots, rotting logs, and saplings
had been left behind. A short but muscular teen guy was waiting for them with a whistle around his neck.

"Who's ready for capture the flag?" he crowed.

Possum cabin was silent.

"Just me, as usual," Sydney called out.

The guy rubbed his forehead. "Uh, this is always a lot easier
with the guys, for sure. Anyway, you know how it works: I
divide you up into two teams, your team chooses where to hide
your flag, and then whoever captures the other team's flag first
wins. And if you get caught, you go to jail, but your teammates
can tag you out of jail." He chuckled. "And you've been hearing this for, like, ten years, so I guess we don't need to go over
it again."

"Actually, Joey, we have a new girl!" Maeve chirped.

Joey looked from girl to girl until he identified Parker,
who wanted to shrink back into herself before she got singled
out any more. "I already know how to play," she lied. The last
thing she wanted was to feel her cabin's disgust build as they
waited for this hyper guy to explain the intricacies of a game
they already hated to someone they weren't going to play with
anyway. No point in team games if your team wasn't going to
trust you.

"Okay, so Cassie is out. Let's do . . . Rosemary, Emma,

Charlotte, and Kaylee on the orange team. Opposing them, we'll have our reigning queen, Sydney, along with Hanna, Zoe, and—what's your name, new girl?"

"Parker."

"And Parker for the purple team. Unless you're secretly a superstar at capture the flag?" This last bit was mortifyingly hopeful.

"Definitely not."

He deflated a bit. "That's okay. Maybe you will be. Who knows?"

The girls were given loose, light jerseys in their team colors that slipped on overhead and smelled like they'd been worn by twenty years of boys who'd never heard of deodorant.

"This is always the worst part." Hanna sniffed her jersey and shook her head in disgust.

"No, the worst part is Sydney going feral," Zoe said, and everyone laughed except Sydney, who snorted and cracked her knuckles.

"It's not the worst thing in the world to care," she snapped. "My team, come on. Let's go." She snatched the purple flag from Joey's hand and stomped off into the woods.

Hanna and Zoe exchanged knowing glances and followed her. Parker was omitted from this exchange and trailed behind. Once they were a good bit away, Joey blew his whistle, and Sydney took off running. The other two girls followed her grudgingly, and Parker struggled to keep up, as running was not her strong suit.

Snark and disdain had been Sydney's main character traits up until today, when running like the wind and barking orders came to the fore. She led her team deep into the woods and stopped when they reached a tall chain-link fence topped with barbed wire.

"Zoe, guard the flag. Rub dirt on it first." Sydney pointed. "Actually, everybody rub dirt on your vest. Try to make it less bright. When it's brown and grungy, put the flag under that log. Hanna, you climb up in that tree and play lookout. Klepto, you're with me." Parker rubbed dirt on her vest but apparently didn't do a good enough job, as Sydney scrounged up a big handful of dark earth and rubbed it all over Parker's vest—and her shirt, just to be a jerk.

Parker was still so out of breath she could barely talk, but she managed to gasp out, "Don't call me Klepto. My name is Parker."

"I really don't care. I'm going to win this, so I just need you to do what I tell you and stay out of the way. And try not to breathe so loud. The whole point is stealth."

When Sydney was satisfied that Zoe and Hanna had done as she'd asked, she hurried into the woods, motioning for Parker to follow her. She wasn't running, though—she was walking carefully, placing each step in such a way that the leaves didn't crunch underfoot. Parker tried to do the same, but every time a twig snapped under her shoe, Sydney shot her a death glare. They were following along the chain-link fence, hunched over behind the underbrush whenever possible, and Parker wasn't sure where they were but knew it was pretty far from Friendship Hall.

Sydney held out her arm, and Parker stopped. Somewhere nearby, they heard footsteps crunching, so they crouched until the noise faded away. While she was frozen, trying to make herself small, Parker had a moment to stare off into the forest behind the fence. The metal was old and dull, except for the bright glint of razor wire along the top.

"Is that to keep people out of camp?" she whispered to Sydney.

"It's to keep campers away from the old campus," Sydney responded. "It's condemned."

"Condemned?"

Sydney heaved an exasperated sigh. "Yes, condemned. They shut it down in the eighties or something, back when my mom went here, but it was going to cost too much to tear it down. Fogarty owns tons of land, so they just fenced it off. I think hunters are allowed to use the north side in the winter or something. Now shut up and come on."

Parker could see dark, hulking shapes far back among the overgrown brush and the tall old trees looming overhead. There was a leaning sort of *T* shape that looked vaguely like the totem pole she'd seen in the old camp photos in the museum. She thought she saw a shadowy figure moving between two cabins, but it was too far away to tell and could've just been a general dizziness from lack of oxygen.

Sydney took off, and Parker had no choice but to follow.

She was totally lost, and her sense of direction was terrible. Sydney moved as if she thought she was a marine, and at one point, Parker had to smother a laugh.

Sydney's head whipped around. "What's so funny?"

"It's just . . . you're taking this really seriously."

"That's because Flag Wars on Friday is really important. Full-camp capture the flag game. I'm always on the winning team. My parents met here, and they were always on the winning team. It's kind of my thing. So stop slowing me down and come on."

They ran some more, and then Sydney froze and put a finger to her lips, dropping to the ground and grabbing Parker's arm to yank her down, too. Pulled off-balance, Parker squawked, "Hey!"

Footsteps pounded in their direction.

"You idiot!" Sydney screeched.

As she stood to run away, she tripped over Parker's leg and fell. Soon a shadow loomed over them, and Kaylee reached down, tagging them both.

"Come on, Queen," she said triumphantly. "Let's get you to a nice, cozy jail cell."

As they followed her, Sydney glared daggers at Parker. "If we lose today, I'm going to get you sent home," she growled.

"It's just a game," Parker responded, bewildered that anyone could care so much.

"Not to me. I don't want you on my team for Flag Wars. I don't care what it takes."

The other team's jail was a wet, slimy crevice between two big rocks. No one tagged Parker and Sydney out. With only Hanna and Zoe left on their team, they lost.

"You're gone," Sydney muttered as the rest of the girls cheered their first victory over Sydney. "First you took our stuff, then Cassie got hurt, then Addison. I'm telling Foggy tonight, and he'll ban you for life."

Parker was used to being ignored or called annoying. She was used to being bullied. But no one had ever looked at her the way Sydney was looking at her.

Like she wished she was dead.

12.

The rest of the afternoon passed in a sort of haze. With Sydney's hate burned into her brain, Parker had given up on being liked or tolerated and now just wanted to be invisible. The only option left was not caring at all. Their next activity was lake time, and while the other girls put on their bathing suits and collected their towels, Parker just sat on her bed with her clipboard and book in her lap.

"You can still have lots of fun in a life jacket," Jasmine said, since Maeve was pretty much avoiding Parker, as if she really were bad luck. "You can swim and jump, go on the inflatables. It's just a life jacket, right?"

"It's mortifying," Parker said, because she was beyond pretending now. "And gross. I'd rather just stay dry and do my own thing."

Jasmine frowned. "You're a hard nut to crack, you know

that? New campers usually integrate pretty quickly, but it's like you're fighting it."

"I'm not fighting it. Everyone else just hates me."

"It's all about attitude—" Jasmine started, and before she could finish with something that sounded like a school counselor's inspirational poster, Parker cut her off.

"Take it from a kid who's been bullied all her life: it's not about my attitude."

Jasmine frowned at her as if she was a puzzle missing too many pieces to solve, so Parker said, "Thanks, anyway," and climbed down off her bed, heading outside with the clipboard and book tucked under her arm.

All the other girls looked like a commercial for a water park as they excitedly talked and laughed on their way down to the lake. They carried towels and beach balls, wore flip-flops and sandals. Maeve had told them that Addison was going to be fine, although she wasn't coming back this year, and they were giddy with relief. Even Cassandra was in a great mood, with a garbage bag taped tightly over her cast so she could join in the fun.

As the rest of the girls ran for the dock, Parker found an old Adirondack chair in a shady spot and set her mind to finishing her latest bracelet. Even if she had no choice but to feel terrible right now, she knew having a new bracelet would at least make Jenny happy. And talking to Jenny would make her happy. All it took was one person who cared, and suddenly the world was a brighter place.

She was taking a break from her bracelet and was fully

immersed in a dramatic chapter of her book when a shadow fell over the page. Looking up, she found Belinda, the lake activities director, frowning down at her from under her visor.

"You got a suit on under that uniform? Let's go do some practice strokes and see if we can get you ready for next year's swim test."

"I don't have my suit," Parker said, holding her place in her book with a finger. "And I'm already a good swimmer."

Belinda's eyes bugged out. "I'd heard you had a bad attitude, but I guess they weren't exaggerating. You know you'd have more fun if you tried to fit in, right?"

And because she was at the end of her rope and knew brown-nosing wouldn't save her, Parker just told her the truth. "I wanted to fit in. I was so excited to come here. I tried really, really hard, and it didn't work. Everyone already hates me. I tell you I can swim; you think I'm lying. I tell everyone Cassandra is bullying me; they think I'm lying. So, yeah, I tried to fit in. Maybe it's time everyone else tried to accept me for who I actually am."

Much to Parker's embarrassment, Belinda squatted down beside her and put her fist under her chin as she made a frowny face. "I know it can seem like everyone is against you, but usually, that means you're being your own worst enemy. I've been here for ten years, and I've never seen a kid who didn't eventually get bitten by the Camp Care bug. You might try talking to Foggy or your counselors, get some tips about how to make friends. I can tell you right now that sitting out during lake time isn't helping. And neither is a constant frown."

The grin Parker gave her was fake and demented. "Is this better?"

Belinda blinked, her pasted-on smile dissolving to a sneer. "Are you disrespecting me, Nelson?"

"No, ma'am. I just don't know what else to do when I feel this terrible and everyone keeps telling me to be happy."

Belinda stood, shaking her head and muttering, "Sheesh. Sorry I tried to help." But then she turned back angrily. "But if you talk to me like that again, I will report you. At Camp Care, we show respect for *everyone*."

As Belinda headed back to her hut, Parker had to dash away a few rogue tears. She was accustomed to being disliked by kids, but she was usually the teacher's pet. The fact that she was now actively talking back and being rude to people in authority made her feel awful. But—well, she kept telling them the truth, and they kept ignoring it in favor of stupid platitudes. Everyone, apparently, had a breaking point, and Parker had found hers. The people of Camp Care did not actually respect her, no matter what Belinda might want to think.

By the time lake time was over, the bracelet was done and Parker had read another chapter of her book, even if her mind had wandered and she couldn't remember a single thing that she'd read.

She slogged through dinner like a zombie, eating outside by herself. Cassandra's injury was old news, but the entire camp was now buzzing with Addison's accident, and the Possum cabin girls were the center of attention. From her perch out-side, Parker could hear everyone talking about it, and it made her sick. She could just imagine Sydney hinting that Parker had had something to do with it, and she was certain Kaylee would no longer correct her. Her suspicions were confirmed when a group of three boys, including Mason, walked past her and one muttered, "Hey, it's the bad-luck Possum!"

"More like a bad-luck skunk!" one of the other boys crowed, and Parker wanted to hang her head and cry as they laughed on their way down the trail. Mason didn't even look back.

A drop of water fell on her cheek, then another on her hand.

It was raining, the gray sky finally giving in to summer showers.

The smell was intoxicating, that marvelous thing her gifted teacher had called petrichor—one of Parker's favorite words. But she enjoyed it for only a moment before realizing that if it rained, campfire time was canceled. Worst of all, she most likely wouldn't get to see Jenny, as they'd probably be stuck in their cabins for the rest of the night.

Maeve appeared in the Friendship Hall doorway, squint-ing through the rain until she spotted Parker. "Come on!" she shouted. "Karaoke time!"

Parker's heart sank. She couldn't imagine a worse fate than full-camp karaoke.

"I'm gonna hit the bathroom first!" she called back. When

Maeve nodded her assent, Parker ran toward the cabins, her book and clipboard held under her shirt so they wouldn't get too wet.

The rain went from a sprinkle to a thunderous gush between one step and the next. Parker put on speed, careful not to slip as the trail grew muddy. She thought about stopping off at the cabin to drop off her book before it got soaked, but she never again wanted to give any of her cabinmates any ammunition against her. Instead, she figured she could leave it on the window ledge in the bathroom and come back for it later. It wasn't hers, after all—it belonged to the camp. And it was such an old, well-worn book that it was unlikely anyone would want to steal it.

She sighed with relief the moment she was inside the bathroom door, her wet sneakers slipping on the tile. It was blessedly dry inside, if a bit dark, and the rain pinging off the roof made it impossible to hear anything else. It felt safe and nice, almost like being in a café. She put the book and clipboard on the ledge, slipped the friendship bracelet in her pocket, did her business, and went to wash her hands at the sink.

"I love storms."

Parker smiled when Jenny appeared in the mirror behind her. "Why?" she asked.

Jenny, soaked to the skin, gazed out the open door. "It's how I feel inside: loud and messy and powerful."

It was an interesting way to think about it. "But you seem so chill on the outside."

Jenny smiled, pleased at that. "They're not the same, though, are they? Not everybody sees the inside. And if they did, they wouldn't like it."

There was a wooden bench built into the wall opposite the shower stalls, and Parker walked over there and sat. It felt protected and private and cozy. Jenny joined her.

"I like how storms change things," Parker said. Something about the way they were alone, separated from the entire camp by the rain, made her feel philosophical. "The world is one way, and then it storms, and afterward, things are different. Sometimes there's a rainbow."

"Sometimes there's a flood."

Parker raised an eyebrow, and Jenny laughed and said, "Okay, but not usually a flood. This one time, lightning struck a tree in our front yard. I saw it happen. It lit up the whole world. It was so pretty. And my dad was so mad, because he knew he would have to pay someone to cut up the tree and haul it away, and then he would have to replace it so there wouldn't be a big hole in the line of trees. But all I could see was what it looked like in that flash. I was so little, I thought the tree might grow back new and beautiful, all covered in flowers, because the lightning was so pretty."

"Did it grow back?"

Jenny looked away. "I don't know. I don't live there anymore."

She said it so sadly that Parker wasn't sure what to say next. Jenny was kind of weird, but people said that about Parker, too.

Needing to fill the silence, she said, "I'm sad we won't have campfire time tonight."

Jenny cocked her head. "Oh. Me too." She grinned mischievously. "But we could sneak out to the dock after lights out. The storm will be over by then, and no one will know."

Parker didn't like it here, but she still didn't want to get in obvious, public trouble and confirm everyone's uncharitable thoughts about her, nor did she want to have to face Foggy— or her parents—regarding rule breaking. Sydney has promised to report Parker to Foggy, but honestly, what was she going to say? That Parker stunk at capture the flag? That she was easy to trip over? She was dreading the moment she was called into his office, but then again, like everything else at Camp Care, it was entirely out of her hands.

"But won't we get in trouble?" she asked.

Jenny shook her head, her legs swinging. "No way. Nobody will know. I've done it loads of times. Please? Please, best friend?"

Parker looked down at the two bracelets on her wrist. She didn't want to disappoint Jenny, but she also didn't want to get caught.

"I don't know . . ."

Jenny held up her pinkie. "Come on."

Reluctantly, Parker hooked her pinkie around it. "Okay. I guess. How will I know what time to go?"

With a little sigh, Jenny looked out the window, the rain

blurring the twilight view of camp as it streaked down the glass. "I'll just be out there already, waiting."

"Parker?"

Jenny hopped up and ducked into the nearest shower stall, so by the time Jasmine stuck her soaking-wet head in the door, it was just Parker sitting there by herself.

"Yeah?"

"Oh. There you are."

"Just waiting for the rain to let up."

Jasmine looked down at her thoroughly soaked uniform. "Well, it hasn't, but I'll get in trouble if I lose track of you. So come on back to the hall. We're going to sing something from *Frozen*."

There was pretty much nothing in the world Parker wanted to do less, but she couldn't think of an excuse, so she got up and followed Jasmine out into the rain. It was letting up, the last orange sunbeams breaking through the dark gray clouds. The conditions were perfect for a rainbow, but apparently no rainbows had gotten that message. The rest of the evening would be gray and miserable, and that was before they got the karaoke machine plugged in.

Parker hid behind her cabinmates through "Let It Go" and "Friend Like Me." She couldn't help noticing that Cassandra had a horrible singing voice but was totally hamming it up, acting like a goober in a way the Cassandra DiVecchio back home would herself ridicule. They exited the stage to mad applause, and Parker slumped over beside Jasmine while all the other cabins did their best—or worst. The boys just screamed and shouted as loud as possible, the little kids tried to sing like pop stars, and everyone else was laughing and clapping and having a wonderful time, but Parker had never been more miserable. Soaked, ignored, doubted. All she had to look forward to was sneaking out to hang with Jenny, and even that caused her anxiety.

That night, she changed into her pajamas as usual and brushed her teeth and did all the normal things a camper would do. She retrieved her clipboard and book and read for a while, retaining nothing. When Jasmine turned out the lights, she curled up facing the door. It took a million years for the rest of the cabin to fall asleep while Parker waited, eyes wide and watering and heart thumping so loud she couldn't believe everyone else couldn't hear it in the utter silence punctuated by the residual raindrops plunking down after the storm.

Finally, when she couldn't stand it a moment longer, she carefully, slowly slid out of her bunk without disturbing Jasmine and crept across the floor. If anyone asked her what she was doing, she would say it was a bathroom emergency. Plenty of people had those. But no one stopped her, and she unhooked the door and stepped outside.

Camp was almost completely dark, except for the lights shining from beside each cabin door on the way to the bathroom. Nothing moved. Orange light glinted off the wet leaves and slick mud. Parker was terrified, both of being in the woods alone at night and of getting in trouble. She went to the bathroom first to pluck up her nerve and make sure no one questioned her. The light over the last stall flickered but didn't go out. After five minutes of staring into the mirror, psyching herself up, she darted down the trail to the lake.

The forest, it turned out, was a different place at night. The darkness wasn't as dark as she'd thought it would be, but the shifting shadows and creeping crackles in the leaves made her feel like a mouse running from a cat. She kept checking the path behind her, kept straining to hear footsteps or someone calling out to her, but nothing happened. She had no idea where Foggy slept, but it had to be nearby. It would be much worse getting caught by him than by one of the counselors.

She rounded a corner and exhaled in relief when she saw the dock. The moon was new and the stars were covered by thick clouds, but still the water managed to glitter and gleam. Down at the end of the dock, a small shadow sat alone, and Parker sped up until she stepped off the dirt and onto the boards. Even though she knew she was a strong swimmer, no matter what Sydney and the lifeguard thought, she knew better than to run on a wet dock.

Jenny didn't look up until Parker was sitting beside her. The other girl was still in her uniform, sitting with her legs crossed. Parker kind of wanted to get her feet wet, but she also knew without a doubt that something had grabbed her, and she couldn't see what was underneath that thick, heavy water, so she put up her knees and hugged them. Her pajama shorts were immediately soaked by the damp wood.

"You came," Jenny said.

"I told you I would."

"I know, but . . ." Jenny trailed off.

"But sometimes people don't do what they say."

"Exactly."

Parker wanted to ask Jenny about what had happened to her, but it seemed very personal to ask someone how they'd been bullied. It wasn't really her business, but she felt that she'd told Jenny a lot more than Jenny had told her.

"Oh! I made something for you," she said, digging around in the pocket of her pajama shorts. She pulled out the bracelet, and Jenny took it and tied it on over all her other ones.

"You're getting better," Jenny noted. "It's beautiful."

"Well, like you said, I ended up back in the art cabin."

They both laughed, but quietly. Sound carried out here. They could hear the birds calling from the forest across the lake, almost as if it was a different, magical world. Somewhere over to the right was the chain-link fence, and there had to be one on the left, but the lake was its own barrier.

"I think I saw some of the old camp today," Parker said.

"That place sucked." Jenny dropped a pebble in the lake. It made a tiny plink and disappeared. "So they say."

"Do you know anything about it? No one will tell me anything. I keep hearing people whisper about how something bad happened a long time ago, and there's someone called Gory Tori, but—"

"We don't talk about that."

"Yeah, that's what I keep hearing."

Jenny tossed in another tiny pebble. "People just need someone to blame when things go wrong. So they make up lies to help themselves feel better. The people in charge ignore it because they want everyone to be happy. They just . . . sweep it right under the rug."

That was definitely true, in Parker's experience, even if it didn't answer this specific question.

"But what happened in 1988?"

It took a long time for Jenny to answer. "The only people who know are the people who were there, I guess."

"It feels like they're covering something up."

Jenny fiddled with her bracelets. "Most people are. But forget about that. It's history. How was your day? What did you do?"

Parker took a deep breath. "My day was awful. You know Addison, the girl who was so mean to me yesterday? She got shot by an arrow. Right in her arm. Nobody knows who did it." She huffed a sigh. "This one girl in my cabin, Sydney, she thinks it was me, even though that's impossible. She thinks I'm bad luck somehow. She said nothing bad ever happened here until I came."

"She's wrong. Bad things always happen here."

"Well, I guess they never happened to the high-and-mighty queens of Possum cabin. Then I made Sydney lose capture the flag, which she really cares about for some reason, and she got so mad that she said she was going to tell the director about me and get me sent home. And I didn't even do anything to deserve it!" A mosquito landed on her leg, and she slapped it hard, leaving a smear of blood.

"Sydney," Jenny said, as if she was chewing on a piece of gristle. "I can't believe she would treat you that way."

"I know! As if I made her trip over me on purpose! The worst part is being accused of things I didn't do. I know the truth, but I can't prove it. It's not like there are security cameras here, or even people with phones. It's just their word against mine, and they're all against me."

"Bad things should happen to bad people," Jenny said quietly.

"Karma," Parker agreed. "And bad things seem to keep happening to the mean girls in my cabin. I'm not saying they deserve it, but—"

"They deserve it." Jenny said it with such fervor and certainty that Parker just stared at her for a minute.

"Addison didn't deserve to get hit with an arrow," Parker reasoned. "But she did deserve to, I don't know, sit in chocolate pudding in the cafeteria and have everybody think she pooped her pants."

Jenny snorted. "That would be pretty funny."

"Right? That's my kind of karma."

"But you can't control what happens. Sometimes people reap what they sow. If the world was fair, they would get what they deserved. This one girl bullied me so badly, I used to just lie in my bunk thinking about the bad things I wished would happen to her. But nothing ever did. She just kept on being pretty and popular forever."

"Yeah, I guess I thought about what it would be like if Sydney impaled herself on a stump, but that wouldn't solve anything. I don't want people to suffer. I just want them to like me. Or maybe . . . not automatically hate me. It's not even that much to ask."

Jenny leaned her shoulder against Parker's. "It's really not. You deserve better."

Parker put her head on Jenny's shoulder. "I'm really glad we met," she said. "If it wasn't for you, I would already be home."

"I'm glad we met, too. You make this place a lot less horrible."

Parker had to pull away and slap at the mosquito on her forehead. "Oh my god, I'm getting eaten alive. These mosquitoes are huge! How are you not covered with them?"

Jenny shrugged. "I guess I don't taste good."

"Well, I hate to say it, but I need to go inside. I'm already starting to swell up. I need to get some anti-itch cream and a Benadryl. Thanks for inviting me out here. It's really pretty. And talking to you made me feel a lot better."

Parker stood, and Jenny looked up, smiling. Jenny really needed to brush her teeth and drag a comb through her tangled hair, but Parker wasn't about to tell her that.

"It makes me feel better, too. Better than I have in a really long time," Jenny said.

"Good night!"

"Good night!"

Parker tiptoed back up the dock, but Jenny stayed there, a quiet shadow perched over the lake. It was nice, sitting out by the water, but Parker was anxious to get back. The mosquito situation was seriously intolerable. It must be really lonely for Jenny here, too, despite the fact that they were both surrounded by their cabinmates and other campers all day and night. Parker wanted to ask Jenny why she kept coming back every year if she hated it so much, but she still wasn't really accustomed to having a friend, and she didn't want to risk making things awkward. Jenny would tell her what she wanted to, when she wanted to, and Parker would just be glad she had someone to talk to at all.

Only when she was safely back in bed with the door locked behind her did Parker realize there was a new, third friendship bracelet on her wrist. She hadn't noticed Jenny tying it on, but there it was anyway.

13.

The next morning was bright and beautiful, and the rest of Possum cabin was excited because Cassandra had sneaked a look at Maeve's schedule and told everyone that they had aerial adventures as their second activity. First, though, they had foraging. Parker expected everyone to groan and grumble, as they had about hiking and wilderness survival, but they all seemed chill with foraging.

Parker soon learned that this was because the foraging instructor was possibly the coolest person she'd ever met: a girl— woman?—in her twenties who looked like Mavis from *Hotel Transylvania*. Her name was Bex, and she wore a big black hat and layers of chokers and necklaces. Even though she was wearing the same Camp Care uniform as everyone else, she gave the impression of wearing all black.

Bex led them deep into the forest, alternating between being quiet and talking about edible plants. Her voice was musical and husky, and she talked like someone in a book, as if she was having an intimate conversation with just you, even if there were eight other people there. The girls asked tons of questions, and instead of ignoring them to focus on her lesson plans or prattling on forever, Bex told them exactly what they wanted to know. It was soothing. Bex could've made millions doing witchy ASMR videos on YouTube.

She showed them different edible berries, pointed out pawpaws and muscadine and meadow garlic, let them nibble dandelion and burdock and clover. She took them into a small cabin surrounded by wild, overgrown gardens and challenged them to taste the difference between peppermint, chocolate mint, spearmint, and catnip. Inside the cabin, bundles of dried herbs hung from the ceiling, and old phonebooks lay open on the table, filled with pressed meadow flowers. They made peppermint tea and talked about how it could soothe the stomach, and she showed them which herbs they could rub on their skin to defy the mosquitoes. Parker was especially interested in this topic and, with Bex's permission, shoved some citronella and spearmint in her pocket for later.

Once they were all rubbed with mosquito repellant plants, Bex led them deeper into the woods to look at mushrooms, but she set out a rule at the beginning: touch nothing.

"These are chanterelles, right?" Cassandra asked, pointing to a cluster of yellowish-orange mushrooms that looked like trumpets.

Bex went over and inspected them. "Probably. But even if

you think you're one hundred percent sure, don't touch. Because as we all know—"

"Never eat mushrooms you find outside without speaking to a professional forager," the group finished for her.

Bex smiled. Her canine teeth were pointed, like a cat's. "Exactly. And even I'm not a professional forager. There are plenty of poisonous mushrooms out here, even some that are poisonous only under certain circumstances. Trust me: it's not worth taking the risk, unless you think you can live without a liver. Now, let me see. If I remember correctly . . ."

She led them through the forest, over a small creek, and to a felled tree with a tall root ball sticking up, where she pointed to a cluster of white mushrooms. "This one is called destroying angel, *Amanita bisporigera,* one of the most poisonous mushrooms in the world. You'd think it would taste bad, that you'd know it was poisonous, but people say it's kinda blah. And then later . . ." She shook her head, bat earrings jangling. "Just don't eat foraged mushrooms."

Deeper in the woods, she showed them slime molds and something called dog vomit that was well-named and a giant fungus that looked like a brain. They found salamanders and a robin's nest with perfect blue eggs and—to Bex's delight, Parker's curiosity, and the absolute horror of everyone else— a tiny black king snake.

"We'll just put this log back down over him," Bex said calmly as the girls shivered and gasped and melodramatically clotted together. "This is his home, not ours. He's not venomous, and he's a lot more scared of you than you are of him. Oh! And look here." She led them all away from the little snake. "Another poisonous mushroom. This one is called autumn skullcap. It's brown and sticky and is often found on old logs. Looks cute and harmless, right? But it's not. It'll kill you. Don't touch it, don't eat it."

It really did look . . . just desperately normal. Parker had thought poisonous mushrooms would be red or bright green, dripping acid like something a witch would offer to a princess. But here they were, just sitting in the forest, looking like something her mom would buy at the farmer's market.

Hiking with Bex was exciting and felt a little bit dangerous, and Parker actually learned things, which she loved. Everyone was too interested in Bex to focus on their dislike of Parker, so it was relaxing, and Parker could almost pretend that everything was normal. But then the xylophone *bing*ed, and Bex led them back to the foraging cabin, where Maeve was waiting.

As they followed Maeve, Parker was at the back, lagging a little behind everyone else as usual. She saw an interesting flower—a trillium, Bex had called it—and stepped off the path to look more closely. Her sneaker sunk into the leaf litter, and something jumped and started shaking.

No.

Not shaking.

Rattling.

She leaped up on instinct, stumbling back onto the trail just in time to see a small brown-splotched snake jerk its head away.

She didn't need Bex to tell her it was probably a rattlesnake. As she watched, it writhed and shook its tail, even struck at the air, nowhere close to Parker's sneaker.

Parker thought about calling Bex back to find out what kind of snake it actually was, but she stopped herself. It would be cool to be the one who found something so unusual and dangerous, but it would just give Sydney and the other girls another reason to blame Parker for their problems. They'd probably never seen a venomous snake here until this one, which meant Possum cabin would have one more reason to call Parker a bad-luck charm.

With one last glance at the snake, she jogged to catch up with her cabin. She didn't tell anyone about what she'd seen. At least nothing bad had happened. But if someone had wandered just a little off the trail, if they hadn't been paying attention, they might be waiting on another ATV right now.

The other campers were amped up about aerial adventures, whatever that was, and Parker had to hurry to keep pace with them. They had to walk a little farther than usual this time, but when the other girls finally broke into a run and Parker looked up, she saw why they were so excited.

Bridges and obstacles made of rope and wood and chain hung everywhere overhead in the tall trees, connecting them like the Ewok village Parker loved from *Star Wars*. There were big platforms, zip lines, and colorful ropes everywhere. Even if she was a little afraid of heights, she reasoned that they wouldn't offer this activity if it wasn't really, really safe.

A team of three counselors wearing harnesses came out, and the leader, Nicole, walked everyone through all the safety procedures.

"Can't we just go? We already know all this!" Hanna pleaded, bouncing on her toes.

"Our new camper doesn't," Nicole said with a smile. "Besides, it's always better to run through it and make sure everyone knows exactly what to do."

Several of the girls glared at Parker, but she was expecting that. It wasn't Nicole's fault, not really, but it would've been great if the counselors could stop pointing at her as the problem. At least training didn't take very long.

Finally she was in her harness and helmet and climbing the ladder up to the first platform. She was the last in line, naturally, and Nicole was right behind her. As soon as Parker reached for the first platform, her stomach just about dropped, and she almost scurried right back down to wait out this activity on the ground. Even if she wasn't generally afraid of heights, and even if there were two safeguards, it was still pretty scary, stepping out into open space for the first time.

Then she saw Sydney and Zoe watching her from the next platform. Sydney was shaking her head in disgust. "Bet she'll chicken out," she murmured.

Parker kept going just to spite her.

Soon she realized how much she loved it. Thinking through each new challenge took up so much energy that she didn't have time to be scared, and because all the other girls were so far ahead, she basically just enjoyed things at her own pace.

This was what she'd imagined when she'd gotten the camp scholarship: doing something new out in nature, something exciting, something a little dangerous.

For a while, she forgot all about Cassandra and Addison and the rest of her cabin. Well, at least until she caught Sydney staring at her or looked down to find Cassandra whining to Maeve about how she could totally do the ropes course with just one arm. But for the most part, it was a great morning, and Parker would've done this activity happily every day.

She got to navigate the ropes course twice, and by the time she was almost done with her second round, the rest of the campers had caught up with her on their third loop, with Sydney in the lead. Nicole was no longer behind her; the counselors had determined that she knew what she was doing, so only the campers were currently on the course.

Whump.

One of the swinging obstacles slammed into Parker's back, a padded roller that looked like a punching bag but was probably more like a big pool noodle. She didn't fall, as she was holding on to two other ropes, but it startled her. When she looked back, Sydney was smirking.

"They call this part the Gauntlet," Sydney said. Stepping forward, she shoved another roller at Parker, narrowly missing her face.

"That doesn't seem safe," Parker said.

Another smirk. "You heard Nicole. It's all perfectly safe. This part is meant to challenge us." This time, Sydney stomped down on the swinging structure Parker was standing on. It was made of boards screwed together in the shape of a big rectangle with an *X* in the middle. Parker wasn't ready, and she got knocked off. For one dizzying moment, she fell, but her safety rope caught her, the harness jerking hard against the insides of her legs.

She looked down at the ground, so far away. It had to be forty feet below her. None of the counselors were paying attention to her at all. Cassandra was watching her, though, looking annoyed as usual, as if Parker just being Parker was an affront to Cassandra's existence.

Parker regained her feet and lumbered off the structure, hurrying around the next tree and the last obstacle before the final zip line. Before, she'd been enjoying herself, but now her body felt like she was being chased by a bear, even if it really was just Sydney and the rest of her cabin. She staggered over the swinging bridges, lurched around the tree, and threw herself down the zip line with more speed than she was used to. On her way, she looked back at Sydney and, much to her own surprise, gave her the finger.

Soon she was climbing out of her harness and handing over her helmet.

"I saw that hand gesture," Nicole said gently. "Be careful. That sort of thing isn't tolerated around here."

"But—"

"But Sydney was goading you. I know. Just remember—she's a legacy here. You're new."

"I don't think I'll be invited back either way."

Nicole's smile was full of pity. "But that's up to how you react to her, isn't it?"

Anger swelled in Parker's chest. Yet again, someone with authority at the antibullying camp was telling her she was reacting badly to being bullied. She muttered, "Thanks," and hurried away before she started crying. Nicole had seen Sydney taunting her . . . and still blamed Parker. All the happiness she'd felt in the trees drained away. Things were back to what passed for normal here.

On the way to the main hall, everyone was in high spirits—except Parker. Not that anyone noticed. They all danced and skipped ahead, some of them linking arms, and Parker trudged behind. She followed them through the cafeteria, took her food, and went outside to eat alone. It was pizza again, and the pizza here was better than it had any right to be, but she felt so awful it was just like chewing rubber.

After tossing her trash, she stood at the nexus where all the trails met. She had a good idea where Foggy's office was, and she thought about what it would feel like to march right up to him and tell him his caring camp was a big lie, a stupid sham, that it sucked and she wanted to call her parents and go home right now. Sydney had sworn she would get Parker kicked out, but so far, nothing had come of it—not that Parker's anxiety could tell the difference.

But then there was Jenny. Parker touched each of her three friendship bracelets, one pink, one blue, and the new purple one, and thought about how Jenny would feel if she got to the campfire tonight and Parker was gone. If this stupid camp made it easier to connect with people outside her cabin, Parker would just go find Jenny and tell her how she felt and get her number or email or something. But she'd forgotten to ask last night, she could never seem to find Jenny around campus, and she wasn't about to ask anybody else for help.

No, she had to stay, at least through tonight. She'd take a pen to campfire time and exchange info with Jenny, and then tomorrow morning she would call her mom and get back to a life where maybe she wasn't liked but at least she knew how to get by. Back home, her loneliness was like a constant weight on her back, pressing down, unrelenting. But here, it felt like she was being chased, hunted, cornered. Like she couldn't quite escape, and every time she got comfortable, she was attacked from a different angle. There, the other kids made fun of her and thought of her as a loser. Here, the other kids actively wished her harm.

But she was willing to stick it out one more night. For Jenny.

Decision made, she sat on a bench to wait for her cabin to emerge from Friendship Hall. Before the xylophone had *bing*ed,

Sydney burst through the doors alone, looking pale and desperate. She ran for the bathroom but didn't make it, hunching over in the grass as she vomited on the ground.

"Are you okay?" Parker asked, getting up.

"Why do you care?" Sydney said between heaves. Before Parker could answer, she shook her head and ran for the bathroom, her hand over her mouth.

Zoe walked out of the cafeteria, looking around. Finding no one else to talk to, she spoke to Parker for, Parker was pretty sure, the first time ever. "Have you seen Sydney? She was acting super weird."

"She barfed and ran for the bathroom." As soon as she pointed at the mess Sydney had left behind, Zoe started to look sick, too.

Without another word, Zoe headed for the bathroom. When the xylophone chimed and the rest of Possum cabin emerged from the cafeteria looking around for their missing cabinmates, Parker told Maeve what had happened. Maeve frowned, which didn't look natural at all on her.

"I've got to go check on her. You guys wait here."

When she left, though, the rest of the cabin followed her, and Parker followed them. They could hear Sydney as soon as they reached the open bathroom door; it was not a pretty sound, and it suggested that she wasn't going to be able to leave the stall anytime soon.

"You okay in there?" Maeve called.

"Go away!" Sydney shouted, followed by a truly horrible noise.

"She's really sick," Zoe said, joining them outside. "It was just barf, but now it's—"

"Do not talk about this!" Sydney bellowed.

They all moved a little bit away.

Maeve looked really worried. "Your next activity is lake time. Why don't you guys . . . um . . . get your suits and change in the cabin? I'm gonna stay here with Sydney."

"But we're worried about her," Zoe said.

Maeve put her arm around Zoe and tugged her close in the sort of gesture that would've looked great on the cover of a brochure. "I know you are. But she would probably like some privacy for . . . this. And I need to walkie Nurse Toby. Sydney won't be able to do activities again until she's gone twenty-four hours without vomiting, so we'll just work on getting her to a cot in the first-aid cabin. She'll be fine. You guys go on, okay?"

All the girls glanced at the bathroom, grimaced at the noises coming from it, and headed slowly for the cabin. They looked so sympathetic, so worried. It had to be great, knowing people felt that way about you. Parker could not relate. She felt bad for Sydney on one level, because she was obviously in the throes of a horrific stomach bug, but on the other hand, it was like what she and Jenny had discussed: maybe it was karma. Sydney had been awful to Parker this whole time, even worse after Addison was gone and Parker had messed up capture the flag. It felt good to know that, for at least a while, Sydney would be way too busy being miserable to worry about being mean to Parker.

Parker got her suit and towel and flip-flops. With the bathroom occupied, the other girls strung up a sheet between two beds to change behind, but Parker was left to awkwardly struggle into her suit on her own, ducked down so no one could see her through the windows. All the way out to the lake, the other girls talked about Sydney.

"But pizza is her favorite food," Hanna said.

"Well, it obviously wasn't food poisoning," Charlotte pointed out. "We all ate exactly the same thing, and it happened before she was even done eating."

"How could it be a virus, though?" Zoe shook her head. "We've all been here together for days. If no one else in camp has a stomach virus, she couldn't possibly catch one. So it has to be food poisoning."

"Or a brain-eating amoeba," Kaylee ventured.

"I heard about those," Hanna murmured. "Can you get them here?"

"It's less likely in temperatures under seventy-seven degrees," Parker offered. When the other girls turned back to stare at her, they didn't look as mean—they looked scared and a little curious. So she went on. "But there's never been a case in this county, and there haven't even been a hundred and fifty cases in the whole world. You mainly just don't want to get warm lake water up your nose." They were still staring. So she smiled. "I checked online before I came here."

"So are we okay to swim?" Cassandra asked—and not in a mean, belittling way.

Everyone was watching, waiting, worried. They weren't looking at Parker like she was the enemy; they were looking at her like they needed her help, like maybe she had a use after all.

"We're totally fine to swim," she said confidently. "Even Hanna would approve of the statistics."

Cassandra shrugged and said, "Good enough for me," before running down the trail with the rest of Possum cabin behind her.

Parker felt the teeniest, tiniest sliver of hope that she might be allowed to fit in . . . but she didn't dare to attempt joining them. She took her time trailing in their wake.

All the other girls dove into the lake and swam out to the floating dock, and it was so hot and muggy that Parker gave in. She grabbed the least nasty life jacket she could find and swam out to the inflatable-obstacle course. With so many kids from so many cabins here, especially so many littles, she blended right in, and nobody bothered her at all. She even helped a couple of little kids navigate the obstacle course in their stinky little life jackets.

When the xylophone rang, for once, Parker wasn't ready to leave. She was having fun, and it turned out that being the only seventh grader willing to help first graders made her super popular. She swam back in with an armada of littles and dropped her jacket off before joining her cabin. Instead of

Maeve, they had Brooke again. All the girls asked about Sydney, but Brooke didn't smile and say she was doing better.

"Just go back to your cabin, change, and chill out," she said ominously. "Director Fogarty needs to talk to everyone individually." She looked around the circle of girls. "We think Sydney might've been poisoned."

14.

The mood in the cabin was silent and oppressive. The girls sat or lay on their beds, pretending to read, but obviously no one could concentrate. They kept stealing glances at Parker. She knew what they were thinking: that maybe she had done something to hurt Sydney or, at the very, very least, that she continued to be the source of their bad luck.

Foggy apparently wanted to speak to them in alphabetical order, which surprised Parker, because, well, she had just assumed that he, like everyone else at camp, would instantly focus on her. Hanna Ames got called first, and Cassandra DiVecchio second. Brooke sat on Jasmine's bed, and every time any of the girls tried to talk, she shushed them. Apparently, there was enough suspicion that they didn't want the girls discussing it or gossiping before their meeting with Foggy. Each time a girl came back, all the others looked up at her expectantly, and then she shrugged and went to her bunk without saying anything.

When it was finally Parker's turn, the stone in her stomach sank even lower. She'd done nothing wrong, and yet she felt as if everyone wanted her to be the obvious guilty party. Then again, considering the way Sydney had been treating her, it made sense that she wouldn't have anything nice to say about the other girl. If they asked her if she actively wished Sydney harm, would she be able to lie and say no?

Because she had wished Sydney harm. She'd said so to Jenny.

She shivered the moment she was outside, despite the scorching weather. It felt like she was being marched to her doom.

Jasmine was waiting there to walk her to Foggy's office. He had a very nice cabin in the forest behind the main hall, near the nurse's cabin. Parker instantly knew it was his; from the outside, it looked like a vacation rental, well-kept and more up-to-date than the campers' cabins, with a nice porch and a swing. Which made sense. Campers came here for a week or a month every summer, whereas the director not only had to be here every day all summer but he also owned the entire campus and all the woods surrounding it. What was he going to do, pitch a canvas tent?

Jasmine held the door open, and Parker walked through. Director Fogarty was sitting at a big wooden desk that looked handmade. The walls were covered with certificates, news-paper clippings, trophies, and professional black-and-white photos of the camp, while a bulletin board behind the desk was covered with layer upon layer of letters and art clearly done by campers. Two chairs sat in front of the big desk. Jasmine sat in one, and Foggy inclined his head toward the other. Parker sat. Thanks to the air-conditioning, the leather was cold and smooth, and her legs immediately stuck to it. She was sweaty, and she wondered if that made her seem guilty.

"Good afternoon, Parker," Foggy said, hands steepled on his desk. In front of him were a lined yellow notepad and a manila folder stuffed with paper, a fancy pen lying alongside. He looked serious and disappointed and maybe like this situation was just as uncomfortable for him as it was for her. "Do you know why we're here?"

"Because Sydney is sick?" Parker answered. She looked to Jasmine, who smiled encouragingly. That was nice—if Jasmine was here, she wasn't alone.

"That's correct. Sydney Williams is at the hospital right now. The doctors think she ingested *Amanita bisporigera*. Do you know what that is?"

Parker nodded. She'd paid close attention to everything Bex said. "Destroying angel mushrooms."

Foggy nodded and wrote something down. "And how did you know that?"

"Well, you had some in a baggie when you were teaching

us survival skills. And we learned about it this morning with Bex in foraging. She showed us some in the forest, on a log."

"And did you touch it or pick any of it?"

Parker drew back, horrified. "Of course not! I don't want to get poisoned. Bex said they make your liver shut down."

Foggy wrote some more and gave a disappointed grunt that made Parker wonder if he'd prefer it if she just acted stupid. Lots of her teachers did.

"Did you know about destroying angels before camp?"

Parker shook her head. "No. I read in a book once that bright red mushrooms are poisonous, but that was it."

"Did you see Sydney displaying any symptoms of illness today?"

That, at least, was a question she could answer honestly.

"Yes. I was sitting outside Friendship Hall during lunch, and she ran out and threw up in the grass. Then she ran to the bathroom, and when the whole cabin went there, she was, uh"—she wasn't sure how to finish the sentence in a true but appropriate way—"going from both ends," she said uncertainly.

Foggy nodded. "And before she vomited, did you see her looking or acting unusual?"

"She was pale when she ran outside," Parker remembered. "I asked her if she was okay, but she screamed at me and ran."

"She screamed at you. Hm. What did she say?" Foggy paused his writing, his pen poised.

"I asked her if she was okay, and she asked me why I cared, and then she ran."

At that, Foggy looked up, eyebrows drawn down. "Does Sydney have reason to think you don't care about her?"

Parker paused. She wasn't here to complain about Sydney; she was here because she was under suspicion of making Sydney sick. Still, if an adult was finally going to ask that question, she was going to answer it whether Sydney was around to defend herself or not.

"Sydney doesn't like me," she said, trying to sound strong but hearing her own voice wobble. "No one in my cabin does, but she's been really mean. She threatened me. She said if I made her lose capture the flag, she'd have me sent home. And she tried to knock me off the aerial obstacle course this morning."

Foggy looked to Jasmine. "I've heard a lot of stories today, and I'm just trying to understand. Is there bullying in Possum cabin?"

Jasmine's mouth fell open, and she looked nervous. "Oh, um, well, as you know, new girls often start out with rocky relationships with established cabins. This week's Possums are a super tight, longtime friend group. But we haven't seen any bullying behavior."

Now it was Parker whose mouth fell open. "Then you haven't been looking." She met Foggy's eyes. She was completely sick of everyone dancing around what was happening to her, just as they did back home. "I go to school with Cassandra DiVecchio. I'm here because I got a scholarship from the school board because she's been cyberbullying me with her two best friends for months. I guess whoever arranged the scholarship didn't know she went here. So when I showed up in the cabin, she told everyone I was a klepto and a liar, then framed me for stealing things. Which obviously I didn't, because how would I know what was important to strangers, and why would I steal stuff and put it in my top drawer? Since then, the whole cabin has hated me. Yesterday, I accidentally made Sydney lose at capture the flag, and she swore she was going to get me kicked out of camp. No one in my cabin will speak to me. I sit alone outside at lunch so I won't have to hear them whispering." She couldn't fight past the tears anymore, and Foggy reached onto his credenza and handed her a box of tissues, looking uncomfortable with her display of emotion. "They're so mean, and all the counselors and Belinda just keep telling me it'll get better, and it doesn't. *It never does.*"

She doubled over, crying, hiding her face with her hands. Foggy and Jasmine were quiet, giving her space, or maybe they were just at a loss for what to say. She wondered if Jasmine and Maeve would get fired for letting her get bullied, and she felt a little bad about that, if so, but she just couldn't take one more minute of being told that she was the one causing all the problems.

"That is a very serious accusation," Foggy said, and it came across so rehearsed that she had to assume it was what he said every time he heard a complaint and needed to give himself time to think.

When he spoke again, his voice was tight. "What you're saying is in direct opposition to what every other girl has told me. I've known Cassie DiVecchio since she was six. Her parents are Camp Care alumni who met here, and generous supporters. Cassie is known for being kind and shy but not a liar. And as for Sydney Williams, I have always applauded her honest, assertive nature and her drive to succeed." Parker looked up through her fingers, and there was no sympathy. Foggy was glaring at her. "Whenever Possum cabin has had a new camper in the past, Sydney has been welcoming and shown great leadership skills. I find it hard to believe that she's capable of the behavior you describe."

Parker looked up, shocked, tears and snot streaming down her face. "But why would I do what Cassandra said I did? Why would I steal? You can call my school and get a copy of my records. I've never even been in trouble before!"

Foggy shook his head. "I've talked to several of your cabinmates, and they've all told me the same story. You have a bad attitude. You stole their things. You lied about it. You said you could swim and then nearly drowned. You ignored safety concerns during horseback riding. You go off on your own when you're supposed to be with your cabin. I think that, in general, you should worry a little less about your cabinmates and a little more about your own behavior. If you want good friends, you need to start by being a good friend."

Parker's head hung. It felt as if she'd been punched in the gut.

"Then just call my parents and send me home. This is the worst week of my life."

Foggy fiddled with his manila envelope. "We don't send campers home unless it's a last resort. My grandparents started this camp to help every kid be their best self. Just because a camper's attitude could use a bit of work doesn't mean we give up on them. I've already talked to your cabinmates about how, here at Camp Care, we give everyone a second chance. So I need you to make a conscious effort. I need you to be a good teammate, to go the extra mile. Try sweeping the cabin in the morning or making someone a friendship bracelet in the craft cabin. Maybe offer someone your pudding."

That made Parker want to bare her teeth and growl at him. Instead, she shook her head.

"I tried that already. Look, just call my parents, okay? I give up. But please—let me talk to my friend Jenny before I leave. She's the only good thing about this place, and I want to get her number or whatever." She slumped down, mopped off her face with a tissue, and stared at the old-fashioned landline phone on Director Fogarty's desk.

But Fogarty didn't pick up the phone. He stared at her like she'd grown a second head.

"Jenny? We don't have a camper named Jenny this week. We have a Jenna, but she's in second grade."

Parker sat up, feeling uneasy. "Jenny. Messy long blond hair. Dark eyes. Freckles. Wears a ton of friendship bracelets and rubber bracelets on both arms. I don't know what cabin she's in, though—I really only see her at campfires. Jenny McAllister."

Foggy abruptly stood, slamming his fist into the desk and sending his folder full of papers flying. He was shaking, his eyes wide. "Is this some kind of sick joke? Who put you up to this?"

Parker scrunched down in her chair. She had no idea why he was so mad.

"No one. I don't—I don't understand."

"I told you. We don't have a camper named Jenny, and the person you've just described—" He broke off and ran a hand through his hair. He was sweating now, his face gone pale. "I don't know what your game is, but I'm beginning to see why you're having a problem here. Go back to your cabin. Try to fit in. And if you see this 'Jenny' person again, you tell a counselor immediately, do you understand me? Immediately!" He pointed at the door.

Jasmine stood and put a hand on Parker's shoulder. "Let's get back to the cabin."

Parker stood, too. Her legs felt wobbly, and all the hairs on her arms were standing up. She ran a finger over her friendship bracelets—the ones Jenny had given her.

"So is she sneaking in illegally or something?" she asked.

"Out!" Foggy roared.

Jasmine guided Parker outside by her shoulders and shut the door gently behind them. Once they were farther away, Parker turned to her.

"What was that? Why was he so mad?"

Jasmine looked just as confused as Parker felt. "I don't know. That didn't happen in any of the other interviews. Whoever your friend Jenny is, she must be trouble."

"But you've seen her, right? We hang out at the campfire together."

Jasmine looked at her just as Foggy had—as if she she'd grown a second head.

"I've only ever seen you sitting alone."

"We sit in the shadows," Parker argued. "She gave me these bracelets!"

Jasmine shrugged. "Okay. You'd know. But . . . like Foggy said, if you see her again, you come tell me immediately, okay?"

Parker had never been more confused about anything in her entire life.

She had a lot of questions for Jenny tonight.

15.

As the last two girls were questioned, Parker could only curl up in her bunk, hiding her head under the covers, her stomach churning. How had Sydney eaten poisonous mushrooms? Had someone given them to her?

Was she going to die?

And what was up with Jenny? Was she sneaking in, or maybe Foggy's memory was just getting, well, *foggy* as he got old and he had forgotten about her? Surely, he couldn't memorize every camper in every cabin, every single week of the summer? Before this, she'd always seen him as kind of an old hippie, just an easygoing but clueless guy who liked singalongs and handing out s'mores and was nice to kids. But whatever she'd said had enraged him. Parker couldn't believe he hadn't just called her mother right then and there.

The more she thought about it, the more she actually *wanted* him to call her mom.

Cassandra had a broken arm. Addison had been shot. Sydney had been poisoned.

Something very dangerous was happening at camp, and all they could do was call people into the office and talk about being good teammates. It was preposterous.

After everyone had been questioned, they went to the main hall for dinner. Jasmine and Maeve had sternly warned the girls not to talk about Sydney . . . which of course meant that they were whispering about her. Everyone in the cafeteria was asking questions and making pronouncements, and Parker quickly began to understand that even without any sort of proof or discussion, the girls of Possum cabin had all agreed to blame her.

She knew this feeling—that weird, rustling silence when everyone was staring at her, whispering about her, snickering behind their hands. She'd felt it every day after the Ice Cream Incident. She dumped her half-eaten food in the trash and walked out to Foggy's cabin. She wasn't liked, and now she didn't feel safe. She was going home, and that was that.

But as she got closer, she could hear him shouting. His door was ajar, and she flattened herself against the wall of his cabin to listen.

"No, I'm telling you she said, 'Jenny McAllister.' I am absolutely, one hundred percent sure we don't have a Jenny this week. Yes, I checked the roster. And the girl she described looked exactly like . . . no, not like Jenny. Like . . . *her*. Messy long blond hair, dark brown eyes, freckles. And those bracelets up both arms. Those photos were never released. You have to know exactly where to look online to find them. Thank God there was no Internet in the eighties."

He paused and kicked his trash can, judging by the loud clank and thump.

"All these years, and we've never had another accident. It was a tragedy, and there's nothing you could've done to stop it, don't get me wrong, but that girl wasn't right, and this isn't right either. I called the real Jenny McAllister, just to see if anyone had been dredging up old stories, but she said there's been nothing." A pause. "She's in her early forties now. She was such a pretty thing, and an ideal camper. And, then, what happened . . . The poor girl."

Parker heard him putting his trash can upright, heard him groan as his knees cracked. He was probably cleaning up his own mess, because he was a good camper, too.

"I know, I know. But it was a long time ago. What happened was terrible, but it's like Mom always said: We have to keep going. We do important work here. We can't save 'em all. It must be somebody sneaking in to mess with us. A prank. Or maybe this new kid is just a bad seed. I've got all the counselors on the lookout, and we'll check the fences, too."

A long pause.

"The hospital is saying it's mushrooms. The white ones. Too early to tell if she'll pull through. Judging by the time she got sick, it would've been at breakfast, maybe even the night before. The whole cabin suggested the same kid might've done it, but nobody can prove anything. She was nowhere close to the sick kid's food. Yeah, a new girl. I know, I know. We're watching her. I'm taking care of it." He sighed. "You, too, Pop. Love you."

As his footsteps neared the door, Parker dove around the corner. Foggy didn't see her, and once he was gone, she hurried back to Friendship Hall. When the xylophone chimed, she was waiting outside for her cabin. She avoided them during the bathroom break and skulked behind them silently to the campfire pit. She took her usual place next to Jasmine, but when she slid off the bench to go find Jenny, Jasmine caught the back of her shirt.

"You need to stay with your cabin," she said.

"But my friend—"

"Dude, come on. There is no Jenny, or else someone is lying to you. You heard Foggy. Just stay here and chill with us. We're not so bad when you give us a chance." But Parker could see it in her eyes: Jasmine didn't think there was any hope. She knew what was happening, and despite her promise to help Parker better integrate, there was nothing she could do. Once the other kids turned on you, there was no way to fix things, and they both knew it.

Parker looked up the hill to the shadows under the trees, but it was impossible to see anything. Jenny might be there, or she might not. She scanned all the other benches, but she'd never seen Jenny with her cabin.

"I'm going to the bathroom—"

"Parker, no. Cut it out. Just sit down and have fun. Be a kid."

Parker wanted to explain that, for one thing, Jasmine was only, like, four years older than her, and for another thing, no kid ever had fun just because someone older commanded them to. But she knew that Jasmine didn't care about her thoughts—or her. She was just an annoyance, the squeaky wheel dripping nasty grease all over the usually sunny Possum cabin.

As the other kids sang campfire songs and went up to toast their s'mores and flirt and take turns in a chicken dance contest, Parker sat on the bench. She felt numb, like she was always outside of the party, looking in as everyone else had fun. Why was she always overthinking things and making bad calculations and saying the wrong thing when other kids just naturally knew what to do? She would've cried if she'd had any tears left. All she wanted to do was talk to Jenny and ask her what was going on. But she couldn't. And she was amazed at how the rest of her remaining cabinmates could just happily goof around by the fire as if nothing was wrong when two girls from their cabin were gone, one seriously injured and one still in the hospital, fighting for her life. It was just . . . a lot of emotions.

After the campfire, Parker trailed her cabinmates through the dark woods, following the bobbing bluish light of Maeve's flashlight. The forest felt cold, the leaves shaking angrily as the tree trunks creaked their complaints. The trip back from campfire time had been so exciting, that first day, but now it felt grim, as if they were far away from everything Parker had ever loved, everything that had ever offered comfort. She wanted her bed and her mom's hugs and her dorky dad quizzing her with trivia over the dinner table. She wanted someone to smile at her—someone solid and dependable who loved her, someone who wasn't random and strange.

She wanted answers from Jenny, but more than that, she just wanted to leave. If nothing else, Jenny had lied to her. Whoever she was, she wasn't actually named Jenny. And if she was trying out a new name over the summer, she should've said so.

As usual, Parker waited for everyone else to clear out of the bathroom before taking her pajamas in there to change. Maybe Jasmine could make her stay on the bench at campfire time, but she at least seemed to understand that, for Parker, now, going to the bathroom with all the other girls would be like throwing chum in a shark pool. Parker went into the first shower stall to change, having mastered the trick of standing on her flip-flops while putting on her pajamas.

She was looking down when a piece of intricately folded paper slid under the shower curtain. Picking it up before it got too wet, she pushed and pulled until she was able to unfold it. In bubbly handwriting, it read:

> Looked like your counselor wouldn't let you hang out during campfire. Totally harsh. I'll be at the dock after curfew if you can sneak out.

The paper wasn't signed. It didn't need to be. Another friendship bracelet was tucked into it, this one in shades of green.

Parker felt a little surge of happiness, just knowing that someone wanted to see her. Maybe Jenny had made up a name, or maybe she was some local kid sneaking in, but she was nice, and she actually liked Parker, and it was really cool that she made friendship bracelets for her. Parker tied on the new one along with her other three. She would go talk to Jenny tonight, ask her the truth about her name, and, depending on how it went, get her cell number or email.

Back in the cabin, the air turned frosty the moment Parker walked in. Everyone stopped chatting, but this time, no one was laughing. It was painfully obvious that two bunks were empty tonight, and for all that Cassandra hadn't been actively bullying Parker and seemed really upset about Addison and Sydney, she certainly wasn't being friendly. Parker climbed into her bed and turned her back to the room, but she was far from sleep. Again she waited until everyone was breathing softly before sliding out of her bunk. She'd already tucked a pen into her pajama pocket to get Jenny's number, so all she had to do was get out the door.

As she unhitched the latch, someone hissed, "What are you doing?"

Parker turned to find Cassandra up on her good elbow, blinking at her like a messed-up baby owl.

"Going to the bathroom."

She didn't need light to know Cassandra was rolling her eyes. "No, you're not. Look, I don't know what you're doing, but no one trusts you. If you get caught, it's not going to look good."

"Why do you care?" Parker whispered back. "You'd love it if I went home."

"Yeah, I would. But everybody is saying you poisoned Sydney, and I know you didn't. And if you get caught sneaking around, they'll think it was you. They'll call the police."

Parker's blood turned to ice at that thought, but honestly— going to the bathroom or the dock was totally normal. If she'd been trying to break into the cafeteria, that would be something completely different. But she had to go see Jenny, and then tomorrow, she'd be gone for good.

"I'm going to the bathroom. My stomach is upset. It's stressful when everyone hates you, but I'm sure you can't remember what that feels like, *Cyclops*." Even though she knew it was babyish and she felt the tiniest bit bad for using Cassandra's past with the eye patch against her, she stuck out her tongue and slipped out the door.

As she hurried out to the bathroom and then to the dock, Parker knew there was a chance Cassandra would wake Maeve and turn her in, but who cared? She was going home anyway. She just had to see Jenny first. If they caught her tonight, she would just get home earlier, and that would be perfectly fine. She'd be in her cozy, comfy, nonrustling, nonmosquito-y bed by dawn.

Sneaking out wasn't as scary as it was the first time. She knew the paths a little better, had memorized the landmarks, and knew some of the trails that branched off and led to other activities. There was enough light to see, and it wasn't as if she was in the deep woods with heavy underbrush, like where she'd seen the rattlesnake and the poisonous mushrooms. That was in an entirely different part of camp. The path to the lake was well-trodden and well-kept, and she was soon slipping off her flip-flops and walking down the dock to where Jenny sat at the very end.

"You came," Jenny said.

Parker sat beside her. "It was a cool note. I love the bracelet. Can you show me how to fold paper like that?"

"I thought everybody knew how."

"Nope. But I can make an origami crane."

"That's rad. I can only do a turtle."

"Um, Jenny." Parker touched a toe to the water and watched the ripples spread. "What's your last name again?"

"McAllister."

"Where do you live? Because I was thinking we could maybe be friends after camp, too."

Jenny looked up. "Do you want my number?" Parker pulled out her pen, and Jenny recited, "555-5112."

"What's the area code?"

"Oh. Um. 404."

Parker nodded excitedly as she wrote the number on the inside of her arm. "Cool. That's Atlanta, right? We're not far away."

"Not too far."

As she was writing, a big mosquito landed on her, and she smashed it. She should've put on bug spray.

"So I have a question," she started.

"Okay . . ."

"Is your name really Jenny?"

Jenny looked away, her messy hair falling over her face. "No. I hate my real name. I hate it so much. I just wanted to try something different."

Relief flooded Parker's chest. She knew that feeling. She'd felt it every time someone had called her Parker Porker or Parker McFarter or any of the hundreds of other cruel nicknames they'd invented over the years.

"Jenny's a pretty name," she said, trying to be supportive. "But I should probably know your real name, too, right?"

"I told you *I hate it*." Jenny's hands were fists on the dock, and Parker could feel her anger radiating out like the ripples in the lake.

"Okay, okay, no big deal. You can just be Jenny to me," she said quickly.

They were quiet for a while until Jenny turned back to her. "Did you have an interesting day today? Did Sydney bother you at all?"

There was a slyness to the question that made Parker uncomfortable.

"Yeah, I guess it was interesting," she answered. "Sydney apparently got poisoned. They think someone gave her bad mushrooms. We saw some in the forest during foraging this morning."

"Is she dead?"

Parker grimaced. Jenny almost sounded as if she was excited by the prospect. "No. She's at the hospital. That's all I know, really. I think the director might send me home soon."

Jenny's head whipped around, her dark eyes blazing. "Why would the director send you home? You didn't do anything wrong."

Parker deflated. This wasn't something she wanted to talk about, but that's what friends did—they talked about the hard things.

"Well, I guess everything was fine before I got here. Then Cassandra got thrown off her horse, Addison got shot with an arrow, Sydney got poisoned. Everyone is saying it's my fault. I guess some people think I'm a freak who did . . . all those things. Other people think I'm a bad-luck charm. The director is saying I just don't fit in, that I'm causing my own problems."

"That's what he always says," Jenny hissed. "And it's not true. He just can't see what's right in front of his face."

"Right? I told him my side of the story, and he basically said it was my cabin's word against mine. So, yeah. I think I'm just going to ask to go home in the morning."

"No!"

Jenny's shout carried across the lake.

Parker winced. "Uh, no, it's okay. I mean, other than you, this place sucks. I want to go home. But we can hang out online—FaceTime or Discord or whatever. Or maybe we could meet at the water park or something."

"No. You can't leave. You're the first person here who's ever cared about me, and I don't want you to go. You have to stay here. If you don't, it's just endless days of the same torture, the same mean girls, the same thing, over and over and over!"

Jenny's voice rose as she spoke, and Parker looked back at the trail.

"We should probably keep it down," she suggested. "I don't want to get caught sneaking out. I'd rather leave on my own terms. I'm not used to being in trouble." She tried to say it in a funny way, but it was like Jenny wasn't listening, wasn't even paying attention. She was staring out across the lake, fingers curled under the dock.

"You said Cassandra was bullying you," she said, her voice low and ominous. "And now she's not. Then it was Addison. She's gone. Then Sydney. She's gone. Who's bullying you now? Who's making you want to leave, Parker? The director? Is he the problem?"

"No. I mean, he's—he's not bullying me. He's trying to help, he's just bad at it. He doesn't like me, but nobody does. I don't know. Just because a couple of bullies disappear doesn't mean everything is suddenly okay."

Jenny growled, low in her throat. "It should. If you get rid of them, the bullies shouldn't be able to hurt you anymore."

All the skin prickled up Parker's neck and down her arms. She swallowed, her throat dry.

"Get rid of them," Jenny had said.

Get rid of them.

"Jenny, did you do something . . . bad?" she asked.

Jenny's head slowly swiveled toward her. "They got what they deserved."

16.

Suddenly, Parker wanted to be as far away from Jenny as possible. It was like playing with a firefly and suddenly realizing it was a wasp.

"I need to get back before someone notices I'm gone," she said, standing up and backing away from the edge of the dock.

Jenny didn't stand. She just sat there, fiddling with her bracelets and staring out across the dark water to the forest on the other side.

"I was trying to help you," Jenny said softly. "They were so mean to you."

Parker took a step backward, then another, watching Jenny as the space between them grew. "That doesn't mean they deserved to get hurt. Or to die." Her voice broke on "die." She didn't like Sydney, but she didn't want this.

"That's because you don't know them like I do, Parker. You don't know what they're capable of. Bullies don't go away on their own. They just get sneakier. They learn how to hide. They learn how to lie. They learn how to get inside you."

Parker stopped. She was shaking, her arms crossed and rippling with goose bumps. "I never wanted anyone to get hurt."

"That's what everyone says. Because it makes them feel less guilty."

Parker was rooted in place, unable to slap away the mosquitoes on her arms and face. She felt like if she looked away from Jenny for a single second, if she so much as blinked, the tension would break and something horrible would happen.

"But I didn't do anything," Parker said.

Jenny looked back at her, her head impossibly turned almost all the way around.

"I did."

Parker shuddered and stumbled backward, almost tripping over a metal dock cleat and falling into the lake. She caught herself and stood.

She remembered pinkie-swearing with Jenny, saying they were best friends. That had been a big, big mistake.

Shaking and hurt and scared and furious, Parker ripped off the four friendship bracelets Jenny had given her and threw them into the lake, where they floated on top of the inky water.

"This is too weird. I don't know who you really are, but I don't want to be friends with you anymore, not if you hurt people."

When Jenny didn't move, Parker turned around and ran

away, feet pounding on the boards, heading for the shore as fast as she could run. She expected to hear Jenny running behind her, or at least shouting at her, and she fled as if she was being chased by a bad guy in a mask in some horror movie. Because that's what Jenny was now, wasn't she? Some sort of monster, a predator, someone willing to hurt other people because—why?

Because she'd decided they deserved it?

Because she thought it would help a friend?

If what Jenny had said was true, then Parker had been hanging out with someone very dangerous. With someone . . . evil.

Jenny had caused Cassandra's horse to buck.

She'd shot Addison with an arrow.

She'd poisoned Sydney.

And now—oh no.

Now she was going to be mad at Parker, too.

Parker had to tell Foggy. She needed to tell him where Jenny was and what she'd admitted to doing. If only she'd had her cell phone, she could've recorded the conversation, and then she would've had proof.

Heart pounding, Parker ran through the forest like her life depended on it. She was out of breath, and she'd left her flip-flops by the dock, and her feet were getting cut and bruised. The trees loomed, dark and rustling, reaching for her with long branches. Pricker vines tore at her legs, and roots snaked out to trip her. Something screamed in the darkness, the sound cutting off abruptly. As she neared the cabins, all the wind chimes went off as if an angry child had struck them, and a door slammed in the bathroom. The entire camp seemed to crouch like a shadowy vulture, cutting off every avenue of escape. At the last minute, Parker changed direction and headed for her cabin, which was closer than Foggy's. She'd tell Jasmine, and then Jasmine would go with her to see the director and she'd have backup. Even if Jasmine didn't believe her—because no one here ever did—at least she'd end up in Foggy's office and be one step closer to going home.

As she got near Possum cabin, she slowed down. Everything looked completely normal, but there was still something eerie about the little building limned in moonlight, the night so still and quiet. She slipped in the cabin door, expecting Cassandra to be awake and waiting to catch her in the act, and maybe the counselors, too. But everyone was peacefully asleep.

"Jasmine," she whispered, putting a hand on her counselor's shoulder. "Jasmine, wake up. It's important."

Jasmine blinked and sat up, frowning. "Parker, what? It's the middle of the night."

"I snuck out and went to the lake and talked to Jenny, and she admitted that she's the one who hurt Cassandra and Addison and Sydney."

But Jasmine didn't bolt up and walkie the director. She didn't even sit up at all. She just rubbed her eyes. "It was probably a nightmare. You're fine. Go back to sleep and we'll talk about it in the morning."

"It wasn't a nightmare!" Parker insisted. "I'm covered in mosquito bites and my flip-flops are by the dock. It happened. You can ask Cassandra. She saw me sneak out."

Jasmine looked over at Cassandra's bunk. "Cassie is asleep. And I'm pretty sure if she saw you breaking a rule, she'd tell Maeve as soon as possible. Back to bed. Now."

Parker glanced back at the door. What if Jenny followed her here? What if she set fire to the cabin or snuck in and stuck a poisoned mushroom in Parker's mouth while she was asleep? Leaving Jasmine, Parker hurried to lock the door. Unsure what else to do, she went to Maeve and shook her shoulder gently.

"Maeve, wake up. I snuck out and Jenny admitted to hurting Cassandra and Addison and Sydney."

Maeve peeked out from under her black eye mask, frowning. "It's just a dream, Parker. Go back to bed. Everything is fine. There's no one at camp named Jenny."

"She told me that's not her real name. Maeve, please. It's not a dream. This is real. I'm really scared."

With a sigh, Maeve took off her eye mask and sat up. She had that sad, pitying look adults give kids when the situation is completely hopeless. "Look, we would've heard it if anyone had sneaked out. Foggy put bells on our door, which is what we do when we have sleepwalkers." She got up, walked to the door, and opened it half an inch. An atonal jangle of jingle bells rang out in the silence, causing several of the sleeping campers to grumble and shift.

Parker pointed at her feet. "Then why are my feet dusty

and bruised? Why am I covered in mosquito bites? Why are all my friendship bracelets gone? And why are you gonna find my flip-flops sitting at the end of the dock tomorrow?"

Maeve shook her head. "Because you're at camp, and those are all perfectly normal things that happen at camp. Look, I get that you're freaked out, but you need to accept that this was just a nightmare. You didn't leave the cabin. Things will look different tomorrow morning. Foggy said you wanted to go home. I don't normally say this, because counselors get in trouble if campers leave for minor reasons, but maybe you should. Camp Care doesn't seem to be a good fit for you."

There was this feeling that Parker knew well now: when nobody believed her and nobody was going to help her, and her only choice was to give up. She knew what had happened, she knew it wasn't a dream, but she couldn't explain how the bells had remained silent when she'd left and returned.

None of it made sense.

And the worst part was that Jenny was dangerous, and nobody believed that part either.

"I think Jenny might try to hurt me," she said in a tiny voice.

Maeve patted her hand and looked at her like she was a sick dog, which did not help. "She can't get to you. The door is locked, and the bells will wake us if anyone tries to get in. You're perfectly safe. Now, for real: go to bed."

Looking utterly exhausted and over it, Maeve gave Parker a gentle shove toward her bunk. Parker trudged over there as if her body weighed a million pounds. As she dragged herself into her bed, Jasmine murmured, "I told you. Just go back to sleep. Everything will be fine in the morning."

Parker knew that was a convenient lie. She knew that none of this would be fine. Her time at Camp Care had been one big nightmare. It wouldn't be fine again until she was home, and even then, it wasn't as if her life had any chance of improving. Back home, she'd still be friendless, and everyone would still make fun of her. Not only that, but Cassandra would have even more social ammunition against her after what had happened here. It was only going to get worse.

She lay in her bed, staring up at the rough boards of the ceiling. How many campers had lain here over the years, feeling scared or sad or angry or homesick? How many people had come to Camp Care hoping to reinvent themselves and make lifelong friends but had instead been carefully bullied in untraceable, unprovable ways? How many kids had been urged into apathetic complacency by their counselors and the director, people whose jobs depended on everybody smiling and being happy?

Probably a lot more than Director Fogarty knew about.

She must've eventually fallen asleep, but it was uneasy slumber, like she was barely balancing and might fall off the bunk at any moment. She woke up several times, expecting to hear the jangle of bells, but didn't. The night was oddly still, the silence ominous. Only after the sun had risen and she couldn't go back to sleep did it occur to her that someone stealthy could just cut open the screens on the door or any of the windows and sneak inside with a lot less fanfare.

When the wake-up trumpet sounded, she felt like a zombie. The bathroom mirror showed hair just as messy as Jenny's, sleepy eyes with smudges underneath, and a bit of a sunburn starting to peel across her nose despite constant application of sunblock. Red, raised, crusty mosquito bites covered her arms and legs and neck and forehead. The number she'd written on the inside of her arm—Jenny's number—was gone. With a creeping sense of dread and unease, she realized she couldn't remember a single digit. She stared in the mirror, unblinking, barely recognizing herself. Whatever was dripping in the last stall in the bathroom had picked up speed, and the light there was dark all the time now. Drip, drip, drip. It was maddening.

She looked miserable and sickly, and even though she brushed her hair out and braided it tightly, she suspected that she did not currently look like the chipper Camp Care Possum she was supposed to be. She wore the uniform, though, and that's what they thought was important—they didn't really care about what was underneath it. They didn't care how she felt—just that she was keeping up appearances for their perfect camp.

After she put up her breakfast tray, Jasmine quietly said, "Do you still want Foggy to call your parents?"

Parker nodded, and Jasmine walked her to the director's cabin. She paused outside his closed door. "Are you sure you want to do this?"

"Yeah. I hate it here. I want to go home."

Jasmine frowned and knocked on the door. Director Fogarty was back in his camp uniform, sitting on the front of his desk with a concerned look pasted on his face.

"Did you even try last night, Parker?"

She looked him directly in the eye. "Yeah. At campfire, I tried to go talk to my only friend—Jenny, who apparently doesn't exist—and was told to stay on the bench with the cabin that hates me. Then I snuck out to talk to my friend on the dock, and she confessed that her name isn't really Jenny and that she's the one who's been hurting people, so I tried to tell my counselors, and they told me it was a nightmare and that I should go back to sleep. Nobody here believes me, so I just want to go home before Jenny tries to hurt me next."

Foggy blinked multiple times, as though if he just blinked enough, she'd disappear and stop causing problems. "Well, maybe you didn't meet us halfway, but it sounds like we did the best we could. It's probably for the best if you go home." He picked up the phone and referred to a Post-it on his desk as he dialed; he'd been hoping for this outcome, Parker realized. She could hear the tinny ringing and waited anxiously for her mom to pick up. Her mom, like everyone else, had her phone with her every hour of every day, usually plugged into a charger so it would always be at 100 percent.

Much to her surprise, the phone rang and rang and was never picked up. Her mom didn't answer, nor did it go to voice mail after six rings, as it should have.

"Maybe she's busy," Foggy murmured. "Shall I try your dad?"

"Okay."

He dialed another number on the Post-it, and the same thing happened. Eternal ringing, no pickup, no voice mail.

Foggy hung up and held the Post-it out to Parker. "Are these numbers correct?"

"Yeah, those are their numbers. Maybe try my grandma?" She wrote Nana Jean's number on the Post-it. As he dialed and waited, her panic rose with every empty ring.

Her mom answered her phone every time, no matter what.

So did her dad.

And her grandmother actually loved talking on the phone and would happily spend fifteen minutes chatting with a tele-marketer.

Yet no one was answering.

The calls all should've gone to voice mail, but that didn't happen either.

A creeping sense of dread shivered up Parker's neck.

"Is something wrong with your phone system?" she asked, as she didn't know much about landlines, and the camp was definitely far away from everything.

Foggy shrugged and dialed another number. A woman's voice answered on the second ring. "Hey, honey," Foggy said. "No, just trying the phone. It's acting up again. Sorry. Love you, too."

He hung up. "Phone system's working fine. Were your parents maybe going on a vacation while you were here? We have lots of campers whose parents travel internationally over the summer, and it can be hard to reach them, what with the time zone changes and phone carrier differences."

"Not that I know of. They both work. And my mom hates planes. She doesn't even have a passport."

Foggy stared at the phone as if he could will it to ring. "There's a neighbor listed on your emergency contacts page. Should I call her?"

Parker's heart sank. Mrs. Miller was an okay neighbor when it came to overpaying Parker to bring in her mail and feed her cats when she was on vacation, but she wasn't any fun to spend time with. When Parker was younger and couldn't stay home alone for too long, she'd had to stay awhile at Mrs. Miller's, where there was nothing to do but sit on a scratchy old couch covered with cat hair and watch soap operas on Mrs. Miller's only TV while Mrs. Miller painted her bulbous toenails.

"I guess."

As the phone rang this time, Parker willed Mrs. Miller not to answer, which she didn't. Again, the phone rang nonstop and voice mail never picked up.

Foggy put down the phone and played with the long, curly cord. "I've got to admit—this is a first. Four contacts, and we can't get a single one on the line. I'll keep trying, and you just stick with your cabin. Jasmine, we'll get Brooke to cover canoeing. You stay with Parker, okay? I think she needs a friend." He gave an encouraging smile that made Parker want to puke. He wasn't pairing her with a friend——he was assigning her a warden.

He stood up and Jasmine stood up, but Parker stayed seated. She had nothing to lose.

"Director Fogarty, I think Jenny is going to try to hurt me like she did the other girls. How are you going to keep me safe?"

Foggy sat back down on the edge of the desk. He was trying to look relaxed, but his fingers dug into the wood edge. "Parker, there is no Jenny. Someone is messing with you. Or maybe you hit your head and didn't tell anybody? I know you had some issues swimming. Do you see a doctor for——uh . . ." He trailed off. "A therapist, maybe?"

"I'm not crazy."

He put his hands up. "Of course not! That's not a word we use here at Camp Care. We know mental health is a complex spectrum, and we want to accept and support our campers as their best selves."

Parker tried not to make a gagging noise. Who talked like that, besides adults trying to cover their butts?

"Then tell me who the real Jenny McAllister is, and why some kid would pretend to be her."

Fogarty stood and stepped back to put his desk between them. He leaned over, bracing himself on the scarred wood. "Jenny McAllister was an ideal camper and is now a gracious donor. She was one of the most popular girls at camp."

"So nothing bad happened to her?"

Fogarty shivered but tried to cover it up with a headshake.

"No, nothing bad happened to Jenny. She was here during a challenging year, but all that is behind us."

Parker put two and two together. "She was here in 1988. And I bet it has something to do Gory Tori."

Foggy stood up tall, towering, turning red with rage. "Get out of my office. Go pack your things. The moment I can get in touch with your emergency contacts, Jasmine will take you to wait on a cot in the nurse's office until your parents arrive."

His jaw was clenched, his eyes bugging out. The air in the small office was suddenly too hot and still, too thick to breathe. Parker could only nod and turn and leave with Jasmine right behind her, pushing her to hurry.

Outside, Parker smiled. She was going home. And she was one step closer to understanding the truth about the real Jenny, Gory Tori, and the mystery of 1988.

Nothing could make Foggy that upset—except the truth.

17.

Jasmine needed to swing by the cabin, so Parker walked beside her, feeling like a dog on a leash. All the other girls were at their first activity, already canoeing with Brooke, so it was quiet and peaceful inside, with a nice breeze and freshly made beds.

Except—wait.

Parker's bed wasn't neatly made, as she'd left it before breakfast. It was all messed up, the blanket and sheets tossed and the pillow half out of its cover and bleeding foam like someone had cut it open with a knife. She hurried to her bunk, furious that Maeve had let the other girls ruin her property in the brief time that she'd been gone.

There on her destroyed pillow were her muddy flip-flops and four friendship bracelets.

The four bracelets she'd torn off her wrist last night and thrown in the lake.

But they weren't wet or stained.

They were clean and fresh, stacked in perfect circles.

Furious, Parker grabbed the bracelets and ran out of the cabin and over to the bathroom. She threw them into the first toilet and flushed it, standing over the swirling water until the bracelets were completely gone. It probably wasn't great for the environment or the camp's septic tank, but she didn't care. Whatever was going on, she wasn't Jenny's friend, and she wanted the evidence of their relationship gone, beyond the reach of anyone who wanted to mess with her.

Jasmine was waiting outside Possum cabin, frantic and calling Parker's name.

"I just went to the bathroom," Parker said.

Jasmine exhaled in relief. "Look, Foggy said I had to stay with you. So you have to stay with me. Just let me know if you need to go, and we'll go together. But if I lose track of you and something happens, it's my job. And unlike you, I love this place."

"Must be nice," Parker grumbled.

As they walked the trails, she could tell that Jasmine was not happy with her. And why would she be? If not for Parker, Possum cabin would've been its usual, happy, perky place, with ten cheerful, well-behaved campers all healthy and accounted for—at least, that's how everyone else saw it. Parker was a problem, a blemish, a thorn infecting a healthy foot.

The other girls had been looking forward to canoeing all week, but Parker no longer cared about anything. She put on her stinky life jacket—at least everybody had to wear one for this activity—and climbed into the last leaky boat. She was in front, with Jasmine in the back. Although she'd never canoed before and had originally looked forward to learning, it was hard to muster any enthusiasm. Everyone else knew what they were doing, laughing as they raced around the lake. Jasmine—who was the regular canoe instructor, after all—told Parker what to do and gently corrected her when she did it wrong, and Parker kept accidentally splashing herself, and her butt was already wet, and the sun was beating down, and . . .

"Do you think Director Fogarty spoke to my parents yet?" she asked.

"He'll radio me when he does. Now, come on, paddle left, now paddle right. We just need to find our rhythm."

"Time to go to the jumping rock!" Brooke called out, and all the other girls cheered. Parker hadn't noticed before now that they were wearing their swimsuits—and Jasmine was wearing hers, too.

"Didn't I tell you to change?" Jasmine asked.

Parker couldn't tell whether Jasmine was being cruel or had just forgotten.

"No."

"I'm sure I did."

Parker could practically feel steam coming out of her ears. "I guess I didn't hear you."

They joined the line of canoes smoothly paddling around a curve to a part of the lake Parker hadn't seen before. There was a big rock out in the middle of water as flat as glass, and near the shore a long knotted rope swayed from an overhanging branch. The other girls tethered their canoes together and took turns jumping off the rock and swinging off the rope, screeching with laughter and cheering each other on. Jasmine joined them as Brooke watched attentively from the rock. It was another picture-perfect brochure moment, and Parker was again on the outside.

"Jump on in," Jasmine called. "Your uniform can get wet."

"She can't. She failed the swimming test," Charlotte reminded her.

Jasmine frowned. "Oh. Right. Yeah, since this is deeper water, you'll need to stay in the canoe for this one. Sorry, Parker."

On the verge of tears, Parker turned away from the scene and gazed across the water to the heavy forest on the other side of the lake. Why did it look more foreboding when it was just a different part of the exact same forest? Somewhere over there, the old camp buildings slowly rotted in the shadows, alone with their memories of the real Jenny McAllister, Gory Tori, and whatever had happened in 1988. Parker couldn't wait to get home and do some Internet searches. It would be so satisfying to learn what Foggy didn't want her to know.

It felt like forever before the girls were paddling back to the shore where the canoes were stored. Parker had forgotten sunscreen, and she could tell her face was as pink as a ham. She helped Jasmine tug in the canoe, took off her life jacket, and followed everyone to the cabin for clothes, to the bathroom to change, back to the cabin. It was all just endless following. The other girls had apparently decided to permanently pretend that Parker didn't exist, and it was a relief. She listened for Jasmine's walkie, for some sign that her parents would rescue her, but it remained silent. She thought about asking to just go wait in the nurse's cabin, but if her parents didn't come pick her up, it would be so embarrassing to rejoin the cabin at the end of the day, almost as if she was publicly admitting that her parents didn't want anything to do with her either.

Their next activity was something called rec games, which was worse than it sounded. They were paired up to play horseshoes, badminton, cornhole, Ping-Pong, and croquet. The only one Parker had any experience with was cornhole, and she wasn't any good at it. The burly teen guy in charge paired her up with Cassandra, and both girls groaned and rolled their eyes.

"Use that on the court," the counselor said, as if there was a big need to channel disgust into croquet.

Parker and Cassandra started with horseshoes. Parker had never played before, and as the counselor excitedly explained the finer points of a good toss, she wanted to throw all the horseshoes in the lake. It was such an annoying game, and she was playing with someone with a broken arm who would probably beat her anyway, because she'd been playing horseshoes since she was a baby.

She took her two horseshoes and stood on the line, then

threw her first one. It fell way short. The next one landed a little closer to the stake. Both of Cassandra's horseshoes also landed short and a little to the side, which was satisfying.

"I'm not left-handed," Casandra grumbled defensively. But now that Parker thought about it, Cassandra hadn't been especially good at any of the activities. She couldn't do rock climbing, she was a terrible singer, and now she stunk at horseshoes. It was nice seeing her nemesis fail.

They walked over to the stake to see whose horseshoes were closer, and it was obviously Parker, but it wasn't really winning: they were both at least a foot away from the stake. She picked up her horseshoes . . . and gave Cassandra hers, too, because it had to suck, having your good arm in a big, bulky cast.

"Thanks," Cassandra muttered. She was up next, and her horseshoes again came nowhere close to garnering a win. "Ugh! God, this is the worst."

"Nice throw," Parker muttered, because honestly, she was just so sick of it all. Of Cassandra's huffy little sighs and aggravated grumbles and eye rolls and complaints.

Cassandra blinked at her. "Excuse me?"

"Well, I just thought the great Cassandra DiVecchio would be super talented at everything at camp because she's been coming here soooo long and everybody loves her soooo much."

"My arm is broken."

"I don't think that's the problem."

Cassandra's jaw dropped, and she actually looked wounded.

"Okay. So I'm not great at horseshoes, and I'm not great at badminton either, when we get to that. Do you want to make fun of my glasses, too?"

Parker opened her mouth, but nothing came out.

Had she just . . . *bullied Cassandra*?

Was that who she was becoming? Is that what Camp Care was doing to her?

She shook her head. "Forget about it. Let's just play."

But when Parker stepped into place, she noticed something wrapped around the stake she'd utterly failed to hit with her horseshoes. It looked like a tangle of bright strings covered in mud . . .

She kneeled down and gently untangled the wad of fiber from around the stake.

It was four friendship bracelets—four very familiar friendship bracelets—blue, pink, green, and purple. At first, Parker thought they were covered in the red clay mud that got tracked everywhere anytime it was wet. But when she looked closer, she saw that it was more reddish, more wet . . .

Like they were covered in blood.

She dropped them and jumped back.

There were red smears on her fingertips.

"What are you doing?" Cassandra asked from behind her.

"Nothing," she said, too quickly.

Parker didn't know what to do—why would her friendship bracelets, which she'd thrown away twice, be here now and covered in blood?

She couldn't tell anyone about this. There was no explanation.

Parker snatched up the bracelets and shoved them down her sock. They were wet and cold against her ankle, and she hoped the red wouldn't bleed through the white fabric. She wanted to run back to the main camp, urge Foggy to try her parents again, hide in her bed. But Jasmine was constantly staring at her, and the walkie hadn't grumbled, and she was stuck here, pulse pounding under the hot sun, hating everything and terrified of what the bracelets might mean. Her next horseshoe throws were even worse, and then she proved absolutely terrible at badminton, cornhole, Ping-Pong, and croquet. All the while, as she tried to pay attention to the counselor's teachings and respond to Cassandra's grumbles, Parker could only think about the friendship bracelets stuffed in her sock. She could feel them pressing against her skin, clammy and unwanted.

Finally, after what felt like hours of Cassandra's huffy silence, the xylophone *bing*ed.

Parker's partner dropped her badminton racket and said, "At least that's over." With one last disgusted headshake, Cassandra left Parker and joined the other girls in their usual clot.

Jasmine had been under a tree with a book all along, looking up constantly to keep an eye on Parker, and Parker could only hope she hadn't seen her pick up the bracelets at the horseshoe pit.

"How'd you like rec games?" Jasmine asked as they followed the rest of the group up the trail toward Friendship Hall.

"Uh, not my favorite," Parker said. As they passed trees and logs and trails, she scanned her surroundings for some way to get rid of the bracelets—for good. She wanted to tie them to a big, heavy rock and throw them into the lake, or maybe poke them down the hole in an old tree. Or—yes. Now she knew what she was going to do. There was one way to get rid of them so that they could never, ever come back.

All through lunch, eaten on the bench with Jasmine, and afternoon activities—juggling and music—Parker was distracted. There wasn't a single moment she wasn't thinking about the friendship bracelets and what it meant that they had returned yet again. She'd thrown them in the lake, she'd flushed them down a toilet, and yet here they were. The only answer was that Jenny—or whoever she really was—kept making more bracelets just to mess with her. They couldn't possibly be the same ones she'd worn. They had to be different; the old ones were gone for good. And where had the blood come from?

Parker didn't want to think about that part.

On the way out to campfire time, Director Fogarty walkied Jasmine to tell her he still hadn't been able to contact Parker's parents, which only made Parker more nervous. They should've answered by now, no matter what they were doing. She could imagine them going out to dinner and getting in a car accident, or maybe there was a gas leak, or—

No. She couldn't think that way. It had to be a problem with the phones. Sure, Foggy could call his wife, but she was probably, like, a mile away at his real house, not four hours away. And if he couldn't reach Grandma or Mrs. Miller, that cinched it. It had to be the camp phones.

"Stay with her at campfire," Foggy reminded Jasmine over the crackling walkie, and Parker cringed at how many people could hear it. "Don't let her out of your sight."

Parker sat on the bench with her cabin and Jasmine. She listlessly mouthed the words to the songs and watched some younger kids perform a play they'd written about talking owls, and when it was time for s'mores, she walked up with Jasmine and stood in line like everyone else. But when she was next, she leaned down as if she was scratching her ankle and threw the bracelets into the flames. She paused to watch them burn, glad to see the embroidery floss spark and catch fire and disappear into black curls.

"Want your s'more?" someone asked, and she wrenched her gaze away and accepted the flaming marshmallow, smashing it between her graham crackers.

Now she would know for sure. If the bracelets showed up again, it was because Jenny was trying to freak her out.

Maybe nobody else believed her about Jenny, but she knew for sure:

Jenny was real, and whatever game she was playing was dangerous.

18.

Again, Parker slept terribly. In her dreams, she ran through the dark forest, chased by some snarling beast with black eyes and fangs dripping blood while all the other campers lined up along the trails to point and laugh. When she startled awake at the trumpet's call, her fingernails had left red imprints in her palms as if she'd held her hands in tight fists all night.

But once they reached Friendship Hall, there was good news: The doctors said Sydney was going to be okay. It would take some time for her liver to heal completely, but they were pretty sure she was out of the woods. The rest of Possum cabin was tearfully joyful, but Parker mostly felt relief. Not because she'd done anything to hurt Sydney, but because she knew that, regardless of the truth, there were many people who would've blamed her if Sydney had taken a turn for the worse. She wondered if this made her a bad person, then reckoned that if you were that worried about being a bad person, you were probably not that terrible.

"We have to win Flag Wars," Kaylee said through her happy tears. "For Sydney."

With all of her problems, Parker had forgotten about Flag Wars—and if she was honest, Sydney was the only person who'd really cared about it before. The rest of Possum cabin wasn't that into capture the flag, and the overall mood was that the boys didn't let the girls do anything interesting anyway. Despite all the camp's songs about equality, apparently when the kids were in the forest alone and winning was on the line, the girls were treated as a waste of time while the boys got to have all the fun.

"What do I do during Flag Wars?" Parker asked Jasmine.

Jasmine slurped up the last of her cereal. "You'll stick with me. Bring a book. Each counselor has to be on patrol, so I'll be out there with my walkie and you'll just chill. I mean, it's not like you wanted to play capture the flag again, right?"

"Not particularly," Parker said, because it was true, but also because she knew that even if she had been free to come and go, her own team didn't trust her and her skills were negligible.

As soon as breakfast was over, everyone went outside. Half the counselors put on fluorescent-yellow vests and melted into the forest, testing their walkies as they sought their posts. Foggy stood on the steps of Friendship Hall and called out the teams. There were ten girl cabins and ten boy cabins, which meant each team had five girl cabins and five boy cabins. It was pretty comical, hearing all the cute, fuzzy-wuzzy forest animal cabin names while watching the boys sneer and threaten to murder each other. Each team was assigned those same purple and orange vests they'd worn at practice with Joey, but they were significantly messier now. Apparently, Sydney's trick of rubbing them in the dirt was a popular strategy. Everyone put on a vest—except Parker. Her team had gotten really good at pretending she didn't exist. Cassandra argued that, even with her broken arm, she should be allowed to play, but Foggy was adamant: she could go out with Maeve to watch the game, but she couldn't participate. She had to give her vest back.

Parker allowed herself a tiny smirk, glad that Cassandra was in the same boat as she was, being embarrassingly babysat by a counselor on the sidelines.

Once everyone was wearing their vests, Foggy gave each team their flag and cleared his throat. The crowd stopped murmuring and focused on him.

"Remember: the boundaries are clearly drawn. Don't go past a fence, don't go past caution tape, don't go past a counselor. Anyone caught out of bounds won't get to play next year." He glared at a boy in the audience who wasn't wearing a vest but whose face had gone bright red. "Isn't that right, Kai?"

"Yes, sir," Kai muttered as the rest of the camp snickered.

"Each team's jail is in the usual place. No rough touches. No grabbing. No tripping. Be kind to our youngest campers.

Kindness is more important than winning. First one to capture the opposing team's flag wins, and then, tonight, it's—"

"Pancake Night!" everyone shouted.

Foggy grinned. "Exactly. Everyone's favorite night. Now, I know I'm forgetting something, but you all know the rules. Go out there and have fun!" He lifted his golden whistle to his lips and blew a shrill blast, and kids exploded into the forest—in opposite directions.

"Well, here we go." Jasmine pulled on her fluorescent-yellow vest and muttered, "East 8 headed to the fence, over," into her walkie.

"Got that. Over," someone replied.

As Director Fogarty walked around, picking up little bits of litter, Parker followed Jasmine down a familiar trail. They passed the foraging cabin, now all locked up, with its wild gardens blowing in the wind. Clouds were creeping in, turning the blue sky gray, and there was an oppressive heat, a pressure in the air, that made Parker wonder about the weather.

"Is it going to rain?" she asked Jasmine.

Jasmine looked up. "Maybe. We're not due for a big storm, though, or Foggy would've postponed Flag Wars. We don't want kids in the woods if there's lightning or strong winds. But don't worry: there are counselors and volunteers all around the perimeter of the game, and also some assigned to hang out near the kids and make sure nothing dangerous happens. Some campers get so caught up in the game they get reckless."

As they walked down the foraging trail, Parker made certain to stay in the center of the path, away from where she'd
seen the rattlesnake—and away from the mushrooms she knew
she'd seen nearby. If she'd been alone, she might've stopped to
look at the patch of destroying angels and see if a few had been
snapped or cut off from the cluster, but there was no way she
was going to so much as glance in their direction with Jasmine
watching her every move. It was a weird feeling, trying not to
look suspicious when she hadn't done anything bad in the first
place, but it turned out that avoiding trouble was inescapable
once people had decided the worst about a person.

Jasmine stopped when they reached the chain-link fence.
The forest beyond looked darker and more mysterious than ever.

"Don't even think about it," Jasmine said.

"What?"

"I see you looking at the old campus. I know you're curious. But it's dangerous over there. Just a bunch of empty old
buildings that might fall down at any moment."

"I don't want to go over there." Parker turned her back to
the fence. "I just wish everyone wasn't so secretive about it. If
people knew the truth, there wouldn't be so many whispers
and stories. But Director Fogarty wants to hide whatever happened."

Jasmine squatted down with her back against a tree and
sighed. "Kids have been talking about Gory Tori since I started
here, and I still don't know what the deal is. I just know some
girl died back in '88, and if you want to get on Foggy's bad

side, all you have to do is bring it up. They say she killed her-self, but that's all I know. Like, it wasn't a camp accident."

"Not like what happened to our cabin this week, you mean?" Parker said icily.

Jasmine shook her head. "I don't know what's going on with that either, but I know full well you didn't have any way to make Sydney eat mushrooms. I was behind you in line that morning. You were barely awake. It was like following a zombie. And then you ate outside by yourself. And Grey says you were behind the line, sitting on the bench, when Addison got shot with that arrow. And Cassandra? Horses are crazy. So I know you didn't do any of that stuff, if that's why you're throwing shade."

"Then why haven't you said anything?" Parker hated how her voice quavered.

"Just because I haven't said anything in front of you doesn't mean I haven't said anything. It doesn't always help."

That was a small comfort—a very small one. Then again, it's not like Jasmine could just tell the younger girls to be nice to Parker and they would. The whole situation was impossible.

Footsteps pounded in the forest, and Parker whipped her head around and saw a gaggle of boys in purple vests running down the path, with two boys in orange vests in hot pursuit.

"What do we do?" she asked Jasmine.

"We just stand here. If they try to go near the fence or do anything dangerous, I blow my whistle." She held up her walkie. "And I can throw out any kids who break the rules."

But the boys just thundered past harmlessly, and Jasmine pulled a book out of her backpack and found a downed tree to sit on.

"This isn't very exciting," Parker said.

"Nope. But it's not supposed to be, for me. I'm at work." Jasmine purposefully picked up her book and held it in front of her face.

Parker found another downed tree nearby and opened her own book, which she'd brought in her backpack, along with a water bottle and a granola bar. The forest was peaceful and quiet when screaming boys weren't stampeding past. As they read in silence, Jasmine's walkie occasionally crackling with news of the game, it became more and more difficult to focus on the words on the page. When Parker looked up, the sky was an impenetrable gray, the clouds roiling.

"Uh, the weather does not look good," she said.

Jasmine squinted at the clouds, gave Parker a doubtful look, and spoke into her walkie. "Home base, how're we looking on the weather, over?"

"We're watching it. Heavy cloud cover, but no rain expected until tonight. No lightning on the radar. Don't worry—its bark is worse than its bite! Hee hee!"

The voice was old and creaky but annoyingly perky. "Who was that?"

"Foggy's dad. He's, like, eighty, and he retired from running the camp years ago, but he never misses Flag Wars. Sitting in that office on his walkie makes him feel twenty again, he always says. Over and over again."

They went back to reading, but Parker couldn't stop constantly looking up. No matter what Jasmine or Foggy's kooky dad said, it looked as if they were about to have a tornado. She could almost feel it, like the same pressure in her ears when she was underwater.

"I'm not feeling so great," she said. "Maybe I could go hang out in Friendship Hall?"

Jasmine's look was pitying. "I know it sucks, but we're stuck here until someone wins or we get called in. It usually only takes two hours. I can't leave my post, and I can't leave you alone. And, hey, if it starts raining, we'll all go in anyway."

Parker began to hope for rain. Not for the part where she got drenched and had to run all the way back to camp, which had to be at least a mile, soaked to the bone, but the part where she took a hot shower and put on fresh clothes and ate pancakes and could finally go to bed, one step closer to this nightmare being over.

"Everybody listen up," the old man said on the walkie, his voice urgent. "We've got a pop-up storm coming in fast. The radar—"

Crack.

Lightning speared down into a nearby tree, blinding the world in a burst of white as thunder cracked so loud that Parker fell to the ground, arms over her head, her book forgotten. A

high, keening screech ripped through the air as the tree top-
pled over slowly, knocking over other trees as flames danced
up and down its trunk. Heavy branches cracked off and fell.
One nearly landed on Parker's head, and she burrowed under
its leaves, hoping for some kind of protection. There was a
single moment of silence, like the forest inhaling, and then rain
fell in one massive sheet, obscuring everything.

"Parker!" Jasmine shouted.

"I'm here!"

"Come on. We've got to get back. This storm—they said it
wouldn't—"

Lightning cracked again, another tree all but exploding before falling with a groan. Parker fought her way out from under
the layers of fallen branches, rain matting down her hair and
sticking her uniform to her skin. Her book was lost somewhere
under all the branches, along with her backpack, but she didn't
care. She just wanted to get out of here, to get back to safety.

But she couldn't reach Jasmine.

The two trees that had fallen—both as tall as she was, even
though they were on their sides now—had blocked her in. Fire
raged along their trunks, too strong for the rain to put it out,
and Parker tried to scramble over the smaller tree but couldn't
get any purchase on the slick bark.

"Parker, come on! Take my hand!"

But Parker didn't see a hand. She didn't see anyone—the
rain was too heavy, the sky too dark, the air too filled with
crackling and smoke. The only direction that wasn't blocked

off was the chain-link fence, and she knew she couldn't climb over it, not with all that razor wire.

But—yes. There was a little place where the fence was pulled up, where an animal had worked at the metal wire until there was just enough room to climb under it. Parker kneeled and dug into the leaf litter, throwing it out of the way to widen the gap. She peeled the fence up as high as it would go and slid her legs under, all the way to her waist. On her back, she held up the fence and wiggled and wiggled and wiggled until she'd made it to the other side.

Here, at least, the trees were still upright. Nothing was on fire. She stood and took a deep breath. Her heart was juddering, she was soaked, her hair was full of leaves and mud, but at least she could breathe again.

"Parker, what are you doing over there?" Jasmine appeared about twenty feet away, bedraggled and shivering, and wrapped her fingers in the fence wires like she could just tear it out of the ground with brute strength.

"I couldn't get out," Parker explained. "But, hey. You need to let go of the fence. If lightning strikes it—"

As if on cue, lightning lit up the sky, and Jasmine danced back from the fence. "Good point. Okay, so walk along the fence, and we'll find a safe place to get you out. I lost my walkie, so we've just got to be smart and stick together."

The rain intensified as they walked along the fence, keeping pace on either side of the twisted metal. Parker was constantly on the lookout for another break or ripple that might let her squeeze back out, but the fence was disappointingly well maintained. Each time lightning flashed, the girls startled and paused, cowering, waiting for the boom of thunder before they began walking again.

"How far does the fence go?" Parker shouted over the pounding rain.

"Miles and miles," Jasmine shouted back. "Foggy's land covers over a thousand acres, but the new campus is only maybe three hundred of those acres."

So he fenced most of it off, Parker thought. The wilderness on this side of the fence spread farther than the camp she was used to, which was so big and tangled with trails that she couldn't figure out where anything was. Even though just a bit of twisted metal was all that separated her from Jasmine and the rest of camp, Parker suddenly felt like she was trapped a million miles away, held apart, as if she might as well be on the moon. She could walk the entire length of this fence and never find another way through it. Foggy might have to show up on the ATV to cut the fence open—but Jasmine would have to leave Parker here alone to make that happen.

"Help!" someone cried. It sounded like a girl, so scared that she was screaming bloody murder. "Help!"

"Do you hear that?" Parker shouted at Jasmine.

Lightning struck and thunder clapped before Jasmine shook her head. "I can barely hear anything."

"Someone is calling for help," Parker shouted back. "It sounds like it's on my side."

"Help! It's bleeding!" the voice called again.

"Which side of the fence are you on?" Parker yelled back.

The only response was a scream.

"Parker, don't—"

But Parker wasn't going to let some unlucky kid die just because she happened to be on the wrong side of the fence.

"Stay here," she told Jasmine. "I'll be right back."

"Parker, you can't, you've got to stay with me! Foggy said—"

Parker shook her head, her hands in fists. "He said I should be a better citizen and try helping the other campers. So just tell him that's what I'm doing."

Jasmine kept shouting at her, but Parker turned away and ran into the forest, toward the screaming kid.

19.

As Parker ran away from Jasmine, the rain seemed to let up just the tiniest bit. The underbrush wasn't as thick, and she could almost see where there had once been trails over here, when it had been a bright, busy camp. For thirty years, this forest had been a summer home to thousands of campers, counselors, and even, she realized, Foggy himself. They'd walked *these* trails under *these* trees, sung songs around their own campfire, and made happy memories that were now commemorated on the walls of the museum. They'd loved it so much that they sent their own kids back to make their own memories.

And now Parker was here, and she was finally doing as Foggy had asked: someone needed help, and she was going to help them.

"Where are you?" she shouted, pausing to listen for an answer.

"I'm here!" came the answering shout.

But where? Parker squinted through the rain and saw something familiar: that crooked *T*-shape she'd noticed the last time she walked through the forest near here, the one that looked so odd and old-fashioned in the ancient black-and-white photos—and, yeah, very culturally appropriated, because no Indigenous people in Georgia had ever made totem poles. She found a muddy path that led uphill toward the cluster of buildings and fought her way past the branches and briars that had grown over the hard-packed trail.

But when she reached the totem pole, there was no one there.

No crying kid, no footprints, no sodden, discarded capture the flag vest.

She cupped her hands around her mouth and shouted, "Where did you go?"

"Inside," the voice came back. "It hurts so much. Please help me! Please!"

Parker beheld the old campus from up close for the first time. It was just like the photos in the museum, except everything was droopy and crooked and falling down. There was a huge hole in the ceiling of the old main hall, the roof collapsing inward as rain poured through and made a lake of the floor. The glass windows were cracked but not shattered, opaque with years of grime and algae and moss. Doors hung open, some missing their knobs. The layout was quite similar to the current campus, with staggered lines of cabins on either side of the hall and smaller cabins and outbuildings marked with

ancient, wood-burned signs. The nurse's cabin just had a big
plus sign, the director's cabin sign read FOGARTY. Those were
off to the side, though. She assumed that the screaming kid
was in one of the closer cabins to the right of the main hall,
judging by where she thought she'd heard the voice.

As she passed by the totem pole, something caught her
eye. A colorful bit of fabric waved gently in the squalling wind
from a carved bird's wing. Every hair on Parker's body stood
up as she plucked the wet friendship bracelet from where it
was caught on the wood.

It wasn't torn, it wasn't bloody, it certainly wasn't burned
to a crisp, but it was pink with a familiar arrow pattern.

It was her old bracelet, or a copy of it. The first one Jenny
had given her.

The one she'd tossed in the lake, flushed down the toilet,
and burned to ashes over the campfire.

And yet here it was, dangling from a sixty-year-old sculp-
ture as if it had been put here mere moments ago.

"Jenny?" Parker called.

The only answer was that same terrified voice: "Please,
help! It won't stop bleeding!"

It was a girl, she was sure now. But was it Jenny?

Parker shoved the bracelet in her pocket and fought
her way through the sleeting rain to the nearest cabin with
a cracked-open door, the one she would've used if she was
lost and alone out here during a storm. Perhaps the cabins
had been painted nicely long ago, but now they were all a

uniform, sun-bleached, rain-wet gray. Lightning lit the sky, arcing down to strike the totem pole in a dazzling bolt. When thunder boomed the next second, Parker felt the ground shake and smelled the sharp scent of ozone and fire. Every hair on her body stood up, and she knew without a doubt that if she didn't get inside one of those buildings, lightning was going to strike her next.

Wishing for a flashlight but desperate to be somewhere safe long enough to regain her wits, she pushed open the old door of the closest cabin. It creaked and swung until it banged against the wall.

"Hello?" she called.

No one answered.

She was about to dart over to the next cabin in between lightning strikes when she noticed that this cabin wasn't actually empty. She'd expected to see the skeletons of old wooden bunk beds, possibly the remains of mattresses long ago robbed of their stuffing by squirrels and time. She'd expected empty dressers with the drawers fallen out and holes rotting in the floorboards. But this cabin—it looked like people had been here recently. Girls, just like in her cabin. The beds were messily made with quilts and unfolded sleeping bags. Camp Care uniforms peeked out of open dresser drawers and were scattered on the floor, just like when the girls got ready for lake time. Old paperbacks were lined up on the windowsills—The Baby-Sitters Club, Sweet Valley High, Judy Blume, Lois Duncan, and some dog-eared Choose Your

Own Adventure. The colors weren't faded with age but bright, as if the girls had just moved in and hurried out to change into their swimsuits. Parker shivered, and not just because she was soaking wet.

One bed was extra messy, like someone had tossed it around on purpose. Parker was drawn to it, almost wanted to set it aright, to ease the wrongness of it. The Care Bears sleeping bag was worn with age and pilling, the pillow torn open, spilling feathers. She reached out to touch the heart on Tenderheart's belly and noticed another pop of color: a light blue friendship bracelet.

Her friendship bracelet.

She snatched it up and stroked it, studying it for any differences that might suggest it wasn't the one Jenny had given her. The only thing she could find was a single burgundy stain, just a little drop, almost as if someone had scratched a mosquito bite while wearing it. She shoved it into her pocket with the pink one and stepped away from the bed, but her foot nudged something under the bottom bunk. She squatted down and retrieved a diary, half hidden by the lower bed's quilt.

There was a little girl in a blue bonnet on the cover, and the lock was busted open. Parker glanced around the cabin as if someone might appear and shout at her for being nosy, but, well, there was no one else here, was there? It almost felt as if she was sleepwalking—she couldn't really stop her hands as they flipped the diary open.

Dear Diary, it began, written in hot pink pen and bubbly letters.

> Camp is horrible. The girls are awful. They said my sleeping bag was babyish, my hair was ugly, and my shoes were from Kmart. Jenny pushed me in the cafeteria, and I fell and splattered the director with spaghetti. I hate her so much. Mom always says that being nice is the best revenge, so I made friendship bracelets for everybody. I'm much better at it than they are. They can only make the little twisty three-color ones, but I can make really nice ones. They laughed at me and threw the bracelets in the campfire. Whoever named this camp got it wrong. No one here is caring. They should've called it Camp Jerk. I wish they were all dead.

Instead of a signed name, there was just a heart, but then again, why would you need to sign your own diary?

Parker ran her finger over the only name: Jenny.

Could that be the real Jenny McAllister?

The one Director Fogarty said was a nice girl and an ideal camper?

She didn't sound nice.

Parker turned to the next page.

Dear Diary,

I take it all back. Jenny apologized and said the girls were really sorry for being so mean to me. She said they were just jealous because new girls get all the attention. They asked me to teach them how to make my friendship bracelets, and they let me sit with them at lunch. I accidentally sat down on a ketchup packet and had to go change, but they were all really nice about it. We did archery today, and I was really good at it—I hit the target every time! Jenny said that if I really wanted to be part of her group with Ashley, Melissa, and Lindsay, I had to go through a special ritual, because they are all blood sisters, and I have to become a blood sister, too. That's why they're all such good friends. I made them each another bracelet, and Jenny said to meet them after curfew at—

The rest of the page looked as if it had been chewed on by rats, and there were no further entries.

She flipped through the book to see if there was anything else, and a key fell out, hitting the floor with a clunk. It was small and silver, but not small enough for the diary—plus, the diary lock was brass. And broken. She stuck the key in her pocket on instinct, because she'd played enough video games and read enough books to know that keys were often useful.

If Parker hadn't lost her backpack in the woods, she would've brought the diary with her. It was history now, and whoever had owned it had to be her mom's age these days. Reading it wasn't being rude—it was learning more about the past. The girl, whoever she was—she had the same problems as Parker. New girl in the cabin, treated badly no matter how nice she tried to be. But at least this girl got an invite to join the inner circle.

Except . . .

No. Bullies don't just change like that for no reason.

Whatever their ritual was, it was probably going to be some mean prank. They were setting her up. Or they *had* set her up.

And maybe . . . that's when something bad happened. Back in 1988.

Or maybe Jasmine was right, and it was just an accident, and the girl who owned the diary couldn't handle it, and . . .

But why was everything still in this room? Why hadn't the girls taken their things home when camp was over? Surely when the camp closed, everyone had time to get their bags out first?

"Help!" the voice screamed again from outside, and Parker dropped the diary and hurried out into the rain.

She was pretty sure now that the voice wasn't actually a lost camper . . .

And yet—wasn't this the mystery she'd been trying to

figure out all along? If she followed the voice, maybe she'd find out what had actually happened here, the reason they'd shut down the old campus.

"Where are you?" she called into the wind.

"I don't know—it's so dark—"

Parker checked the next cabin, but when she swung the door open, the back wall was caving in, the room entirely taken over by the storm. There was nothing but decaying wood inside, no mattresses or blankets. The next two cabins were the same, just empty gray boxes with rough bunks made of two-by-fours, falling down like a big game of Jenga. The fifth cabin was leaning at an impossible angle, and Parker worried that if she touched the door, the whole thing would just collapse.

The bathroom was next, built in the same style as the one at the current campus. Instead of a door, there was just an open breezeway, with ripped-out screened windows set high up on the walls. When she stepped under the overhang to get out of the rain for a moment and listen, it felt like she was in a cave.

"Hello?" she called, but no one answered, and she was very glad to leave. With so few windows, it was impossible for light to reach past the overhang. The bathroom felt like a shipping container, like a heavy box that might suddenly entrap her. She was almost certain that if it hadn't been raining, she would've heard a familiar dripping, way back in the last toilet stall.

Out beyond the bathroom, she saw two more buildings that she couldn't quite identify. They were built similarly to the cabins, but one had pipes coming out of the top and sides and a big padlock on the door. The padlock was shiny and silver and looked as if it might've been put on yesterday, whereas everything else here looked its age. That was the building farthest from everything else.

The first mystery building was some sort of storage shed, with rough wood shelves and piles of rusted old trash: a soup can, a bicycle pump, a pocketknife, what was left of the rim of a basketball hoop. Everything was in shades of gray and brown except for a strand of bright green wrapped around the pocketknife handle. Parker was not surprised to find a friendship bracelet there. As she unfolded the knife to pull it free, rusty red smeared across her wet hands, dripping down her fingers.

"Ha ha," she mumbled, as if trying to deny the frantic thumping of her heart.

The bracelet was wet and stained red where it had touched the knife, and Parker snapped the knife shut before she could risk cutting herself on the blade. She'd had her tetanus shot after stepping on an old nail, but she'd read up on what it meant to die from lockjaw and wasn't taking any chances. She shoved the dirty bracelet in her pocket with the other two, trying hard not to think about how everything that was happening was impossible, and she was still missing one more bracelet.

The storm outside had not lessened a bit, although the lightning, thank goodness, seemed to have moved away. The rain whipped nearly sideways, driving Parker toward the last structure, the one with the padlock.

"Hello?" she called.

"Hello?" someone responded—from the other side of the door.

20.

A fist pounded on the door, and someone screamed, "Let me out!"

Parker ran around the shed, but there were no other doors, and the only window was high up in back and too small for a person to fit through. She had to get that door open. Shivering in the rain, she held the lock in her hand. It was shiny silver, both modern and new. It was the only thing here that didn't fit with the rest of the abandoned camp—well, except for the friendship bracelets, which had been left for her to find, whether as a trail or a taunt. Maybe she should go back to the storage shed and get the knife and try to jimmy the lock, since she didn't have the—

Ah.

The key from the diary.

Of course.

Parker pulled it out of her pocket and rubbed the red stain

from the bracelets off on her shorts. It looked like blood and it felt like blood, but she didn't want to think about that. There was so much she didn't want to think about—couldn't let herself think about. So much of what had happened this week didn't make any sense, and yet she was helpless to escape. She felt as if she was in the eye of the hurricane, trapped, surrounded on all sides by danger but forced to move in a very particular path.

That path had led her here, to this lock. It had given her the key.

She had to find out who was behind the door.

She stuck the key in the lock and turned it, and the lock popped open. It was a tight fit, but once she had the lock off the latch, the door creaked open.

"Hello?" she said again.

"Oh my god, Parker?"

As she stared into the darkness, someone shoved her, hard, from behind. She stumbled into the room, and the moment both her feet were on the boards, the door slammed shut behind her. She spun and felt for the doorknob, but—there wasn't one. It wasn't that kind of door.

"Don't bother. You can't open it. Believe me—I've tried."

Now stuck in the small space, Parker was forced to confront the other occupant:

Cassandra DiVecchio.

She sat against the wall, her wrists tied together with an old piece of rope.

Well—her wrist and her cast. It didn't look comfortable.

"Cassandra? What are you doing here? Are you the one who called for help?"

By the scant light shining through a single dirty window near the ceiling, Parker saw Cassandra roll her eyes. "Yeah, obviously. I need help. This is so messed up."

"But you said you were hurt, that you were bleeding—"

Cassandra shook her head. "Nope. I just called for help."

"How'd you get here? And who did this?"

Cassandra was trying to play it cool, but she was shaking, her face wet with tears. She was a total wreck. "I don't know. There's no one else here. I haven't seen anyone else. I was out on referee duty with Maeve. We were near the fence, and then the storm started. A big tree fell on the fence, and I got blocked into this weird space and had to climb over to get away. It—it sounds like it doesn't make any sense, but it does. I got separated from Maeve, and then something knocked me out—a falling branch, I think? And I woke up here. Where are we?"

Parker swallowed hard. "We're in the old camp."

Glancing around, Cassandra grimaced. "Okay, that explains a lot. So were we . . . kidnapped?"

"I don't think so. I found my own way here. But there's been a lot of weird stuff going on." She stood over Cassandra, looking down at her, noticing her bedraggled hair, red-rimmed eyes, crooked glasses, and runny nose, worlds away from the Cassandra she knew back home. "Do you know anything about what happened here in 1988?"

"We're not supposed to talk about that."

Parker gestured to the shack around them, with its rusted-out water heaters and pipes. "Look around! Foggy's not here! No one is! The Bad Camper Police aren't going to show up and bust you. You are literally where it happened, so just tell me what you know."

Cassandra looked down, fought with her ropes a little bit. Parker reached over and plucked at the frayed strands until the other girl was freed. Wrapped up with the rope was the last friendship bracelet. Parker automatically stuck it in her pocket.

"Thanks. That hurt." Cassandra rubbed her wrist, where the skin was red. "Okay, so . . . I don't even know why it matters, but my mom was here when it happened. There was this new girl in her cabin, this super weird girl named Tori, and she was totally obsessed with my mom, like she wouldn't leave her alone. And when she didn't get the attention she wanted . . ." She paused and had to look away. "She killed herself."

"That's a lie."

The voice that had spoken—it wasn't Parker or Cassandra. But it was familiar.

It was Jenny.

21.

A shape stepped out from behind the rusted hulks of tanks and pipes and machinery.

"Who are you?" Cassandra asked, scrambling to her feet and moving to stand by Parker.

"Jenny," Parker whispered.

Cassandra was scared, but she was angry, too. "There's no Jenny at camp. I've never seen her before. What's she doing here?"

"You didn't see her sitting with me at the campfire?"

Cassandra shook her head. "You were always alone."

"Well, I guess you have to see me now," Jenny said in a weird singsong voice.

There wasn't much light, but Parker could see her ex-friend now, looking the same as ever. Same mussed blond hair, same freckles, same dark eyes, same knockoff Keds, same legions of bracelets up each arm. But Jenny wasn't smiling. And she was pale—too pale.

For a long moment, Jenny didn't say anything. There was just an odd, dripping noise, almost threatening, like an attic leak that might lead to a flood.

Like the drip in the last stall of the bathroom.

Drip.

Drip.

Drip.

"Jenny, what is this—" Parker started.

"That's not really my name," the girl said. "I wish it was, though."

Parker understood now. "You're Gory Tori."

The other girl nodded. "You can just say Tori, you know. They told me my name was weird. They told me a lot of things."

"And Jenny . . ." Parker's teeth wanted to chatter, but she fought it. "That was your diary, wasn't it? Jenny McAllister was the girl who bullied you." She looked to Cassandra. "Are you saying Jenny McAllister *is your mom*?"

"Yes, but she's lying!" Cassandra shouted, glancing swiftly from Tori to Parker. "My mom said Tori was the bully. That she kept trying to force everybody to be her friend. That she had no boundaries. That she wouldn't take no for an answer. That she was creepy and weird and a stalker and would do anything for attention."

Parker kicked Cassandra's foot and shook her head. Making Jenny—no, Tori, Gory Tori, the camp ghost—

Making her angry wasn't going to help anybody.

"She was a bully!" Tori shrieked back. "She was mean! She called me names and made me sit on ketchup and told everybody it was my first period. She ran my bra up the flagpole, she and her clique. I tried so hard to be nice. I gave them my cookies at lunch and made them friendship bracelets and swept the cabin every morning and made their beds, but they were still mean to me. Until . . ."

Tori swayed as she spoke, her voice high and quavering. "Jenny said they'd changed their minds. That I'd proved I was a good friend, but if I wanted to truly fit in, I had to become a blood sister to her and her three best friends, the most popular girls in camp. They told me the ritual would take place on Friday night—right here, the boiler room cabin, because nobody ever went there. Jenny said I had to go inside at midnight and use chalk to draw a circle on the floor, and I had to sit there and make a little cut on each wrist to prove my loyalty, and then they would all come in and join me and we'd touch our cuts together and be bound by blood forever."

"That's messed up," Parker murmured, but Tori wasn't listening. Cassandra grabbed her wrist, hard, tears streaming down her face.

"So I did. I made friendship bracelets for each of them, and I drew my circle and used the pocketknife Jenny gave me to make teeny little cuts exactly how she told me to."

Tori held up her left arm and pulled back the layers of bracelets to show a deep, red cut longways on her wrist. Blood dripped down to her elbow and puddled on the floor. She did the same with her right arm to show the same red-rimmed wound.

Drip.

Drip.

Drip.

"I did exactly what she said," Tori whispered. "And I waited. And they never came. It was so cold. And the blood came too fast. It wouldn't stop. When I tried to leave and go to the nurse's cabin, the boiler room door was locked."

Parker followed Tori's line of sight to the back of the door. It was covered in scratches and smeared with blood. A fingernail was caught between two boards.

"I died here," Tori said. "And so will you."

22.

Cassandra threw herself at the door, screaming for help, but Parker wasn't about to turn her back on Tori. They obviously weren't getting out the same way she'd come in, so there had to be another way.

"I thought you said we'd be best friends," Parker said.

Tori's glare went dark. "And then you said we weren't friends anymore."

"Because you hurt people! Sydney and Addison and—" She looked at Cassandra, who was trying to wedge her fingers in the door.

"I hurt the people who bullied you the same way I wish someone had hurt the people who bullied me."

Cassandra spun around, furious. "I didn't bully anyone!"

Parker's jaw dropped. "Are you kidding? Have you forgotten the Ice Cream Incident? *You* did that. The only reason I'm here at all is because you and your friends bullied me so bad that the school board gave me a scholarship to convince my parents not to sue!"

Cassandra had the grace to look ashamed. "Look, I . . . I didn't know they were going to do that, okay? I forgot you were coming over, and they were already there. KJ decided to hide in the closet to listen in, and then she texted me and said to take you downstairs. I didn't know what she was going to do."

"But you didn't stop her! You just stood there and watched!"

"And I felt horrible about it! I still do! You don't know what it's like—being popular."

Tori snickered.

"No, I don't," Parker said sharply. "I only know what it's like being unpopular and bullied. Because of you."

Cassandra slumped against the door, dashing tears away with her good hand. "You don't understand. Before we moved, I got bullied all the time at my old school. Kids broke my glasses and made fun of the eye patch I had to wear. They called me Cyclops—and so did you, for all that you pretend you're so innocent. And they called me other names. Nothing great rhymes with Cassie, okay? One girl snapped my violin bow on purpose. This camp—my old Girl Scout troop from back home—they were the only ones who really saw me, really liked me." She looked up, furious. "That's why I needed you to go home. If they found out what happened at our school, if they knew the kind of stuff KJ and Olivia make me do—"

"They wouldn't want to be your friend," Parker finished for her. She sniffled and wiped at her nose. "Pretty funny, that you bullied me to keep them from thinking you were a bully. It'd be real funny if I wasn't the victim."

"It'd be great if I didn't feel horrible all the time," Cassandra added softly. "I swear, I've had stomach cramps all week." She looked up, and Parker saw a glimmer of the girl underneath Cassandra's hard shell, the girl she'd laughed with over ice cream. "I'm sorry. For everything. I always wanted to be popular, and once I was, things got out of hand."

"It's not that easy, though," Parker argued. "I mean, I could maybe try to understand what it's like, with KJ and Olivia. Last week, if they'd told me to jump off a cliff, I probably would have. I tried to change my entire personality just so people would like me. But here, once we were at camp? You could've just been nice to me, and it would've been the best day of my life, and I never would've told anyone here anything about back home. But you doubled down. You just made it worse."

Cassandra's head hung. "I know. I thought that if I just told them you were bad news, they wouldn't believe you. But then they wanted proof, and I needed to make sure, and I put that stuff in your drawer, and . . . it got out of control. If I could take it all back, I would. I was desperate. If I lost Possum cabin . . . it would be like I didn't have a single real friend in the whole world."

Parker made eye contact. Both of them were crying.

"That's how I feel every day of my life, Cassandra. Home, and here. Every day. Because of you."

Much to Parker's surprise, Cassandra pulled her into a hug

and buried her face in Parker's shoulder. "I'm so sorry, Parker. I'm so sorry. It's the worst thing I've ever done. You don't deserve it."

Parker was crying, too. "I know I don't."

"You're actually pretty cool. I had more fun eating ice cream with you than I ever did with KJ and Olivia."

The feeling in Parker's chest—it was as if she'd held her hand in a fist for months and this was the first time she'd relaxed her fingers. The tears came hard, and she clung to Cassandra and let it all come out.

"I needed to hear that so badly," she whispered into the mess of Cassandra's hair.

"Can you ever forgive me?"

Parker pulled back and looked at Cassandra. Not the perfect, diamond-hard school version of Cassandra DiVecchio, but Cassie, the messy camper who wanted the same thing Parker did—friends—and had clearly gone too far and lost sight of what really mattered.

"I can try. If you'll promise to come clean with Possum cabin. And just . . . be nice to me."

Cassandra's lip trembled. "They're going to hate me—"

"Not if they're the good friends you think they are. Real friends can forgive each other."

Cassandra shook her head and exhaled. "Yeah, I guess they can. I really messed up, huh?"

"Yeah, you really did."

"I'm just going to keep apologizing, probably. It's such a relief, coming clean."

Parker smiled—a real smile. "Then I'm sorry I told a ghost I was mad at you and she got you thrown off a horse."

For a moment, the only sound was quiet chuckles and sniffles with a background of pattering rain and the steady drip from Tori's arms.

Because—well, with all the Cassandra stuff, Parker had kind of forgotten why they were here.

She'd forgotten they were trapped with a ghost.

She turned to face Tori, whose fingers played up and down the bracelets on her bloody wrists. "Aren't you going to attack us? Why are you letting us argue and cry like this?"

Tori grinned, showing black-rimmed teeth. "Because it's funny. Because I've got nothing better to do. And because you're trapped here, just like me. You can do whatever you want. Scream, cry, argue, apologize. None of it matters. You don't matter. Camp doesn't care about you, just like it didn't care about me. No one will hear you, and you'll slowly rot here until you die. Jenny McAllister will finally get to feel some of the pain she put out into the world . . ." She held out a blood-wet pinkie. "And you and I will really be best friends forever."

23.

Parker did not hook her finger around Tori's. She did not want to die here. She wouldn't. There had to be some way out. There was always a way out.

"Maybe I could stand on your shoulders and climb out," she said to Cassandra as she looked up at the narrow window.

"I can't hold you up with a broken arm."

"Okay, then I can hold you up."

"But my arm—"

"What, are you going to break it *more*? This is an emergency."

They tried several methods of getting Cassandra up to the window, but Parker just wasn't strong enough, and Cassandra's balance was off. The window didn't open—it was firm, thick glass. When they looked around the room, they couldn't find anything they could use to smash it open. Everything left in the room had rotted or rusted away to nothing, all the pipes as thin as paper and the water heaters too rusted to hold any weight. Even Cassandra's cast was soggy from being out in the rain.

"I told you," Tori reminded them. "You can't leave."

"Why would we believe you?" Parker shot back. "You're a ghost."

Cassandra finally turned away from the door, her finger-tips bleeding and a hopeless look in her eyes. "The door won't budge. All these run-down buildings, and this one is solid as a rock."

"They don't make 'em like this anymore," Tori chimed in. She was sitting on the floor with her back against the wall now, playing with her bracelets. Other than the ones Parker had given her, they were stained an old, rusty red with blood, but otherwise, Tori looked like any other camper, albeit a little messy, a little . . . off. Parker couldn't believe she'd once sat beside her, clutched pinkies with her, told her most personal stories to a vengeful ghost.

But—something was keeping Tori here, allowed her to take form.

Was there some way to get rid of her? To send her back to—wherever she was supposed to be? What held her here, besides the desire for revenge against those who'd hurt her?

They couldn't get out through the door or window, and the walls were solid. Parker looked down at the floor. There was something there, a heavy white line on the graying wood boards. It had to be the chalk circle Tori had drawn, as bright and powdery as the day she stood here, young and hopeful and alive, fully believing that all her dreams were finally coming true and she'd soon be one of the popular girls.

Parker scrubbed a foot through the chalk line, and Tori looked up, pained, and put a hand over her eye.

"Stop!" Tori shouted.

"Cassandra, we have to erase the chalk line!" Parker shouted.

Cassandra's head shot up, and together they rubbed their sneakers through the chalk. Tori screamed for them to stop, jumped up and grabbed Parker's hair and tried to pull her away, but Parker just shoved her, hard. Her body felt like a ham, like something heavy and wet and dead, and Tori landed on the floor with a thick, squelchy *thunk*. When she stood, Parker almost threw up.

It was as if parts of Tori were . . . rotting.

Her dark eyes were going white and filmy. Her lips were peeling away, curling back like an old jack-o'-lantern. Her hair was drying up and falling out in chunks. Her tan summer skin had bleached out to pale white threaded with lavender veins, and her fingertips were shredded meat gone black around the edges.

"Keep going!" Parker urged Cassandra.

The ghost—the corpse—whatever Tori was now—pulled and tugged at them, pummeled and screeched and tried to stop them, but the more of the chalk line they erased, the weaker Tori became. By the time they'd moved all the way around the circle, she was fading away.

"You can't get rid of me," Tori growled. "We'll be here to-gether forever."

Parker hated to admit that she was right. Even if Tori was less solid, even if she no longer felt like a threat, they were still trapped in a tiny cabin with her, with neither water nor food, and the door was firmly locked from the outside. Even if Parker still had the key, it wouldn't help. She stuck her hands in her pockets and found . . .

The four friendship bracelets.

She'd worn them proudly, then tried to get rid of them, but they'd stubbornly kept coming back.

There had to be something important about them.

Were they the ones Tori made for the four girls who should've been her blood sisters?

Was that what kept Tori rooted here—that promise that was never fulfilled? That ritual?

She glanced at Cassandra's fingers, which were already bleeding. Then she gritted her teeth and reached down, press-ing her thumb against a big splinter in the wooden floorboards. A bead of blood welled up, and she stood.

"Tori, do you still want to be blood sisters?" she asked. She held out her thumb, dripping blood perched on its tip. "Come on, Cassandra. You, too."

Cassandra shot her a glance that said this was a very bad idea, but apparently living life under KJ and Olivia had made her more likely to just do what she was told. Cassandra held out one of her fingers, a smear of blood dribbling from where she'd been prying at the door.

Tori gasped.

"Really?"

She was nearly see-through now but when she looked at their offered hands, she changed. It was almost like a sunbeam breaking through dark clouds as she grew more corporeal and less . . . decomposed. She stepped toward them, and if Parker squinted just right, Tori could've been just another Camp Care kid in her uniform, her hair a little messy and her hands covered in red clay. Her smile was hopeful, her eyes shining.

"Really," Parker answered.

"That's all I ever wanted," Tori whispered.

She reached her left hand out to Cassandra and her right hand out to Parker, and Parker and Cassandra each reached out both of their hands so they would make a circle. Cassandra's hand slid into Parker's and squeezed reassuringly. Parker was terrified she'd have to touch the place where—where Tori had hurt herself—but Tori just put her thumb against Parker's, a cold, clammy kiss like touching a frog.

And then, between one blink and the next, Tori was gone.

24.

"Where'd she go?" Cassandra asked.

Parker looked around the small room, barely a shack. Light shone in the window overhead, the sun finally fighting past the heavy cloud cover as the storm moved off. They were still plagued by the sound of dripping water, but it was only the trees shedding rain. The floor wore old stains, rusty brown and dull white, but the wet red puddles that had formed around Tori were gone. When Parker tried the door again, it pushed right open.

They stepped outside, nearly falling onto the muddy ground. Cassandra was crying softly, but Parker was mesmerized by the ruins of the old camp. In the pouring rain, it had seemed foreboding, big and dangerous and abandoned. Now it looked sad and homely, smaller than she would've imagined. Faded caution tape floated on the breeze near the cabin where she'd found the diary, and when she peeked inside, it was utterly changed. There were no colorful blankets, no Care Bears sleeping bag, no books lined up on the windowsill. There were only old, broken beds and graying wood falling down, gravity tugging everything closer to the grave.

When Parker started walking back the way she'd come, Cassandra followed. They passed by the totem pole, its paint faded, a black streak showing where lightning had once struck it.

"I can't believe my mom used to go here," Cassandra said. "Like, she probably walked right here. Her feet touched this ground."

"I can't believe your mom bullied Tori to death," Parker said, because she was done pretending that horrible things just happened and she was supposed to accept them and move on. She was sick of the way everyone tried to just sweep the bad stuff under the rug and forget about it.

"I know," Cassandra said, her voice tiny. "Her version of the story was . . . different."

"Suicide. They called it suicide. But it wasn't."

"No, it wasn't. My mom did something really, really horrible. Maybe she didn't know it would turn out as bad as it did, but . . ." Cassandra shivered. "I never want to make someone feel that horrible."

"Poor Tori."

Parker reached in her pocket and touched the friendship bracelets there. She wasn't ready to look at them, certainly didn't want to wear them, but they felt like . . . not a gift but more like a reminder. All Tori had wanted was friends, just one friend, even. If one person had reached out to her, if one person had defended her, even if one person had stopped Jenny from her cruel prank, Tori might be alive right now.

Maybe she'd been annoying, or desperate, or needy, but she hadn't deserved to die like that.

She'd walked here, too. She'd been here, at summer camp, surrounded by hundreds of other kids, and she'd felt horribly, awfully, hopelessly alone. Just like Parker.

"Cassandra! Parker!" someone called.

Parker shook her head— she'd been so wrapped up in, well, everything that she'd forgotten they were lost on the forbidden side of camp.

"Over here! We're over here!"

Cassandra urged Parker to stay by the totem pole, as one of the things they'd learned in Foggy's survival class was that when you were lost, it was better to stay in one place where you could be seen rather than roaming around all over the place. The grass was still beaded with rain, and there was nowhere to sit, and Parker realized that she was completely exhausted. It was only afternoon, but it felt like she'd been awake all night and running for her life. She was still soaking wet, and the afternoon had cooled off from the rain but was swiftly heating back up.

As the voices called for them, they called back.

"Sure would be nice to go for a swim right now," Cassandra said.

"Definitely. Even if I have to wear a gross life jacket."

Cassandra turned to her, head bowed. "Uh, so I have another confession to make. I dared one of the boys from Groundhog cabin to swim under the dock and grab your foot. It was just supposed to be a joke. I didn't think you'd freak out like that."

Parker's jaw dropped. "Are you serious? And this whole time, you never just, like, pulled Maeve aside and told her?"

Cassandra looked away. "No. Everyone here likes me and thinks I'm nice. I was afraid that if I told the truth, they'd turn on me." She sighed. "But I'll tell Maeve. It's just . . . it's not worth it. None of it. I don't want to be popular anymore. Not like I am back home. But the girls in our cabin know the real me. And they deserve the truth."

Parker shook her head. She'd lost so much time to Cassandra's lies. "You're diabolical."

"At least you already forgave me?" When Parker raised her eyebrows, Cassandra added, "I know, I know. I'm going to come clean. I promise. And I'm done with KJ and Olivia. Things are going to change."

Maeve and Jasmine appeared in the forest, and Parker and Cassandra waved and jumped up and down before running to meet them. Maeve and Cassandra hugged and cried all over each other, and Jasmine hip-bumped Parker.

"You scared me to death," she said.

"I was pretty scared, too," Parker admitted.

They all walked back to where the tree had fallen over the fence. It wasn't climbable from this side, but Foggy was waiting with two ATVs and some bolt cutters. He'd had part of the fence ripped open already and put down the cutters as soon as he saw the girls returning.

He mopped his sweating forehead with a handkerchief. "You girls know you're not allowed over here," he said, clearly upset.

"It was the only way to get away from the lightning, Director Fogarty," Cassandra said. "I was hurt, and Parker had to get me somewhere safe. I got hit on the head, and she saved my life. We're sorry. We didn't have a choice."

Parker stared at Cassandra, who looked like a perfect little angel. They hadn't discussed what story they were going to tell when someone asked them what had happened, but apparently Cassandra had decided for herself.

"And sir—Parker didn't do anything wrong this week. I spread a rumor about her. I didn't follow the Camp Care way. It's my fault she's had all these problems. She didn't hurt anyone or steal anything."

Foggy looked as if he had never been so surprised and disappointed in his entire life. "Cassie, that doesn't sound like you at all."

"It really doesn't," Maeve added, shocked.

"I know. I made some bad decisions. I'm sorry. I want to make up for it."

Foggy looked from Cassandra to Parker as if he was trying to conjure the truth out of thin air. "Well, this sounds like something we could discuss further once we're all back at camp. Cassie, you've been a model camper your entire life. I think your mother is going to be quite surprised to hear about what you've done."

Cassandra's head hung, but her eyes blazed. "I'm sure she made mistakes, too, sir."

Before Foggy could talk about what a perfect camper Jenny McAllister had been, Parker said, "You don't have to invite me back, sir. But please let Cassandra keep coming here. I know it means the world to her."

Cassandra's face lit up with hope, and she gave Parker a grateful look. Parker couldn't quite believe it herself— Cassandra had been true to her word. She'd told the truth in front of Maeve and Foggy, even though she might lose the thing she loved most. They were on the same side now, helping each other.

Then again, when they'd become blood sisters with Tori, they'd been holding hands, too.

According to the rules, they were blood sisters for life.

25.

The ride back to camp was bumpy and uncomfortable. Maeve gave each girl a rough blanket, but that was kind of the opposite of helpful, since they were damp and the afternoon was steamy. Jasmine told them about how all the counselors had had to round up the campers and get them into Friendship Hall to wait out the storm, and they'd found everyone except Cassandra and Parker. Search parties had been out for hours with ATVs and bullhorns, looking for them. For the first time in Camp Care history, Flag Wars was considered a draw. Foggy's dad was still grumpy about it and demanded a retry tomorrow, but Foggy had put his foot down.

They were taken to the nurse's tent first to be checked out and have their wounds bandaged and Cassandra's cast redone. With the storm gone as swiftly as it had arrived, the rest of the kids had been given the choice of going to the lake or hanging out in their cabins, so most of the kids were at the lake.

The girls of Possum cabin, however, came running once they heard that Cassandra was back. They swarmed around her as she and Parker walked to Friendship Hall, asking to sign her new—if kinda ugly—white cast and ignoring Parker completely. For a moment, Parker felt that familiar sinking stone in her belly, that sad understanding that she was being purposefully excluded. But then Cassandra stopped walking.

"Guys, I think you got off on the wrong foot with Parker—" she started.

"Because of what you told us," Charlotte said, casting Parker a dirty glare.

"Well, I was wrong. She's not a thief or a liar. She didn't steal anything. She goes to my new school, and I . . ." Cassandra paused, her face gone red and her eyes wet behind her glasses. "I haven't been very nice to her back home. And I didn't want you guys to know I was kind of a mean girl, so I told you to stay away from her, and . . ." She gulped and sniffled. "I'm just really sorry. Parker's actually nice, okay? She's cool. And she saved my life tonight. So just be nice to her."

"So you're saying . . . *you* lied to us?" Hanna asked, incredulous.

"And stole our stuff?" Zoe added.

Cassandra nodded. "I'm really sorry. I messed up big time."

The girls of Possum cabin looked from each other to Cassandra to Parker, unsure. With Addison and Sydney gone and Cassandra now admitting to her deception, no one seemed to know who to follow.

"Let's go to the lake," Charlotte said to the other girls. "We need to talk about this. See you later, Cassie. And Parker." She nodded at Parker as if just seeing her for the first time and led the other girls toward the cabin.

On their own again, Parker and Cassandra went into Friendship Hall, where they were treated to their own personal early Pancake Night as they sat across from each other at their usual table. They were quiet, but it was a friendly, thoughtful sort of quiet. They'd been through something huge, something impossible, something they could never fully explain to anyone else. And Cassandra, of course, had her own new problems to wrestle with. Maybe the girls of Possum cabin would forgive her, and maybe they wouldn't. Still, it was a relief. Camp no longer felt quite as threatening to Parker— it was just a place, and the campers were what brought it to life.

"You should come back," Cassandra said out of nowhere.

"I don't think I can. Foggy hates me, and I was a scholarship kid anyway. And . . . well, maybe they won't let you come back either. Foggy seemed pretty mad."

Cassandra smiled, a crooked, sweet smile very unlike the one she used at school. "I mean, as you know, my parents are big donors. And . . ." She nervously crumbled up her cookie. "It kinda feels like my mom owes you? Us? Someone? It just seems like the right thing to do. If you wanted to come back."

Parker looked out the open double doors to where two girls

were throwing a Frisbee. "If I tried it again, would I be in the same cabin, and would you be nice to me? Would the other girls be nice to either of us? All week, I was so lonely, but I kept thinking that if I just had a friend or two, it would be the best place ever." She looked down. "That's why I started hanging out with her—with Tori. When she was Jenny. She was alone, too. She understood. She was nice, before she tried to kill us."

"Yeah, I think I'm done being popular. It's not as much fun as it looks. Did you know KJ makes all her friends go with her to have their eyebrows waxed? It was the most painful thing I've ever felt."

"And you got thrown off a horse by a ghost!"

They laughed together, because it sounded impossible but they both knew it was true.

Director Fogarty walked in and raised a tufted eyebrow at their frenetic cackling, but then again, it's not like a sixty-something-year-old guy could possibly understand the mind of a recently haunted twelve-year-old girl. "Parker, we finally got in touch with your mom. She's on her way. You'll need to go pack your things. She should be here before dark."

Parker glanced at Cassandra and looked down, feeling shy. "But . . . I kind of want to stay now."

Foggy pinched the bridge of his nose, looking as if he'd aged a decade since breakfast. "Well, the last I heard, you really wanted to leave. She's already on her way. There's only one full day left this week anyway. At least you got your pancakes."

"Yes, sir," she said, a bit deflated. "Thank you."

He left for his office, and Cassandra stood with her tray. "If we hurry, we have enough time to play on the inflatable obstacle course."

Parker stood, too, but she didn't pick up her tray.

"That would be cool. I just need to do something real quick."

As she walked to the museum, she pulled the tangle of friendship bracelets out of her pocket. They were slightly damp, a little stained, and to her surprise, old and faded. When she'd worn these bracelets, they'd looked like they'd been made the day before. Now they looked their age:

Thirty-four years old.

The lights were off in the museum, the afternoon sunbeams gilding the taxidermied animals in shades of russet and gold. It took Parker a moment to find just the right place, but suddenly she knew. Where 1987 ended and 1989 began, between pictures of the old camp and the new camp, she stuck a pushpin borrowed from the map through the wall and hung up the four bracelets. Maybe Foggy would notice it, maybe he wouldn't, but this is where they belonged.

Camp Care could try to forget what had happened in 1988, but Tori deserved to be remembered. Not as she was whispered about, a vengeful, bloody figure that stalked the night, but as a girl who'd been misunderstood, bullied, and ignored. She should be remembered—so it would never happen again.

When Parker returned to the cafeteria, wiping the tears off her cheeks, Cassandra was dumping out her tray for her.

"Thanks," Parker said.

Cassandra grinned. "Sure. That's what friends do."

DELILAH S. DAWSON thought she would be a visual artist but somehow ended up a writer. She has worked as a muralist, an art teacher, a barista, a reptile caretaker, a project manager, and a dead body in a haunted house, which was probably the most fun. She is the *New York Times* bestselling author of *Star Wars: Phasma,* the Minecraft Mob Squad series, *Mine,* and seventeen other books for kids, teens, and adults, as well as the comics *Ladycastle, Sparrowhawk,* and *Star Pig.* She loves gluten-free cake, adventures, the beach, Disney World, and vintage My Little Pony. She went to one week of overnight camp in 1988, and it was so terrible that it inspired this book.

WHIMSYDARK.COM